She caught sight o
clothing.

"Olive!" Kayla shouted. "Olive, are you there?" Kayla rushed past Nicolas into the motel room. "I have to find my sister."

Nicolas appeared at her side. "We will find her. Let me check the man on the ground." A few long strides brought him to the foot of one of the beds. He glanced down and rubbed the back of his neck.

In that instant, she knew the opportunity to make amends with her father had ended. She swayed on her feet. *I have to see Trevor for myself.* Once next to Nicolas, she leaned into his solid body. Her vision blurred with tears. Even a man like Trevor didn't deserve to die like this.

"I'm sorry I didn't get here sooner." One tear slid down her cheek. Regret mixed with grief.

"If you'd been here, you would have been hurt, too." Nicolas stroked her back.

"Or killed." She swallowed the lump in her throat. If Olive had been in the motel room with Trevor, had they hurt her? Taken her with them? If Trevor's murderer was searching for valuable jewelry, then what use was a little girl?

Kayla stepped forward and away from Nicolas's soothing touch. His concern was touching, but she couldn't allow distraction. Not with her father dead and her sister missing. Olive might be in the crosshairs of a murderer...

Multiple award-winning author **Laurie Winter** is a true warrior of the heart. Inspired by her dreams, she creates authentic characters who overcome the odds and find true love.

She enjoys time with her family, who are scattered between Wisconsin and Michigan. Laurie has three kids and one fantastic husband, all who inspire her to chase her dreams.

SAFEGUARDING THE WITNESS

LAURIE WINTER

LOVE INSPIRED

INSPIRATIONAL ROMANCE

LOVE INSPIRED®
INSPIRATIONAL ROMANCE

Recycling programs for this product may not exist in your area.

ISBN-13: 978-1-335-49844-1

Safeguarding the Witness

Love Inspired
22 Adelaide St. West, 41st Floor
Toronto, Ontario M5H 4E3, Canada
www.LoveInspired.com

Printed in U.S.A.

But they that wait upon the Lord shall renew their strength; they shall mount up with wings as eagles; they shall run, and not be weary; and they shall walk, and not faint.

—*Isaiah* 40:31

My writing is inspired by my wonderful family. Thank you with all my heart.

With gratitude to my agent and all-around fantastic person, Jana Hansen; editor Adrienne Macintosh, whose expertise helped craft a story I love; and editor Johanna Raisanen who offered my proposal for *Safeguarding the Witness* the gift of joining the Harlequin family.

ONE

Something was very wrong. Hesitating outside the rear door of her father's house because it was ajar, Kayla Swartz reread his final text—Come over as soon as you get into town. Hurry. I need you to take care of your sister. She wasn't on good terms with Trevor, her estranged father, and hadn't been since her childhood. But they'd begun speaking again after her half sister had come to live with their father a year ago. Mostly to ensure the three-year-old child was being cared for. Trevor's track record as a dad up until then hadn't been great.

Yesterday, he'd called, begging her to take the little girl because he had gotten into trouble—again. Instead of enjoying spring break, a week off from teaching high school art, she'd hopped into her car and rushed north.

But now worry grew. She pressed her palm against her stomach, fighting a swell of uneasiness. The back door was left open, so either Trevor was still inside, or he'd left in a hurry. Her golden retriever, Sasha, stood patiently behind her, waiting for Kayla's next move.

Sasha was a trained therapy dog, which came in handy when entering the hospital room of a sick child but not so much when walking into a risky situation.

The potential for danger wouldn't have crossed her mind if not for Trevor's criminal history. He'd been in and out of jail since she could remember. And if not for her little sister, she wouldn't have raced to his house first thing since crossing the city limits of Snowberry, Montana, after a long drive from Colorado Springs. Once she had Olive, she planned to head to her mom's house and celebrate Easter, which was this coming Sunday. If Trevor had gotten himself into a mess, then that mess was his own. Kayla wished to spare an innocent little girl from experiencing the same trauma she had with Trevor Swartz as a father.

She called him again, and it went to voicemail. Maybe she should call the sheriff's department. After a moment of contemplation, she decided to go inside and assess the situation before involving a deputy who might arrest Trevor simply on the basis of his reputation for trouble.

Kayla checked the view through the doorway and found no movement or activity. She entered, and her eyes took a moment to adjust to the low light. Standing in the kitchen, she froze. The wreckage surrounding her stole the air from her lungs. Every cabinet door was flung open; a few barely hung on their hinges. Food, dishes and cookware covered the vinyl flooring. Something definitely was not right. She inhaled, taking in the familiar scents of cedar and decades of cigarette smoke. Something else lingered in the air—the faint odor of men's cologne. Definitely not a scent related to Trevor, but it nudged the back of her mind.

Sasha barked and dashed off toward the living room, tail wagging. Her dog had never met a person she didn't immediately love. Then again, she hadn't met someone with evil intentions.

Kayla chased the dog, then skidded to a halt at the sight of the tall, broad-shouldered, dark haired man staring back. *I should have grabbed a knife.* Her fear eased, though, as she realized the man looked familiar. A quick inventory of the living room showed it wasn't in any better condition than the kitchen. "What are you doing here? Where's Trevor? Did you make this mess?"

"Whoa." He held up his large hands, palms facing out. His jaw clenched. "Slow down."

She'd seen those dark brown eyes before. Recognition struck like an electric shock. During high school, Kayla had stared into those same brown depths when she should have been helping him solve algebra equations. "Nicolas Galanis. What are you doing here?"

He was taller and wider than he'd been in high school. Back then, she assumed that he couldn't gain any more height or muscle, or that his jaw couldn't become any more chiseled. The years had been kind. Nicolas had been handsome as a teenager. Now he was dangerously gorgeous.

Gaze narrowed, he studied her face, then softened his hard expression. "Kayla. I'm glad it's you."

He remembered her. Then again, how could he forget her? His relationship with Kayla was the reason Nicolas lost his football scholarship. Déjà vu played through her mind, and her gut sickened. Their romance had been young, innocent and sweet—and punctuated by a tragic ending. The last time she'd been with Nicolas, they'd been on a date. They'd gotten ice cream at a downtown shop, then walked hand in hand on the sidewalk lost in conversation. Shouting stole their attention, and they made their way to a nearby tavern, where they found Kayla's father engaged in a brawl. Trevor had been tossed to the ground, losing the fight and calling for help, when Nicolas stepped in. She'd spent every day since regretting his involvement. Which begged the question: Why was he here now?

She crossed her arms over her body. "Trevor asked me to come to Snowberry and stop by his house. He said he was in trouble and needed me to take my sister. Have you seen either one of them?"

Nicolas crept forward, stepping around sofa cushions, side table drawers, and miscellaneous junk strewn over the carpet. "No one was here when I came by. I came home to spend some time with my family for the holiday. It's a long story, but Trevor reached out last year and we've stayed in touch. He texted me a little while ago, asking if I could come over to check on his house and you. The back door was left open, so I stepped inside. I was here for only a minute before you arrived."

Staring at him, she blinked while attempting to make sense of his words. Nicolas and Trevor were in contact? That made no sense. If anyone had as much reason to hate Trevor as Kayla did, it was Nicolas. After his dashed dreams of playing football in college and beyond, Nicolas enlisted in the army. Her young heart had broken when he left without a word of farewell. Then again, she never should have hoped for more. A popular athlete and a nerdy art student didn't have much in common outside of the library study room. She'd been lucky Nicolas had asked her out in the first place. Her fantasy of a future with him had crashed down around her that horrible night almost fifteen years ago. If Nicolas had made amends with Trevor, perhaps he'd forgive her as well.

"Did Trevor mention what's going on?" she asked, still processing the news that Trevor had gone to Nicolas for help too.

"Wish I knew." He bent over to rub Sasha on the head. "When was the last you heard from Trevor?"

"About two hours ago." Kayla checked the time. She'd been driving through the mountains when her phone picked up a cell signal. It had taken her a little while longer to locate a pull-off spot to check her text messages. What she read chilled her more than the cold Montana wind. "He asked me to hurry. Now he and my sister are gone and the house is trashed." And her high school crush was standing in the living room. Painful memories stirred.

"Do you know where he may have gone?" His question hung in the air.

She had little notion of Trevor's life these days. Their relationship had been severed after a childhood of trauma and humiliation. Being known around town as Trevor Swartz's kid had been a heavy weight to carry around as a girl, and she'd moved away at the first opportunity. "No." She shook her head. "We're not close. You remember what he was like. The man was—probably still is—a criminal." As a child, she'd had no choice but to attend the court-mandated visits. Finally, those visits were stopped. All Trevor added to her life was constant disappointment. Thankfully, she had a wonderful mom who balanced out her father's shortcomings.

Which led her thoughts back to Olive—the reason she'd reconnected with her father and the reason she was here. Her half sister's mom had signed away her parental rights a year ago, leaving Trevor with sole custody. The child deserved better than what she'd gotten from life so far.

"People change." Nicolas approached the picture window and pulled back the curtain to gaze outside. A dusting of snow still covered the front yard. "He's not the same person."

People like Trevor don't change.

A doll with a head full of yellow yarn hair lay on the carpet. Kayla rescued the poor thing and set it upright on a chair. "You can go. You should go. I'll call the sheriff's department to report a break-in. Someone was here looking for something."

"Wait." He surveyed the room. "Let me keep trying to get a hold of Trevor. I don't want to get him in trouble if there's a simple explanation for what's going on."

A simple explanation? Doubtful. "Try calling him then." Protecting Trevor was low on her list of priorities, but locating Olive remained her top concern. Nicolas was right; they should at least try once more. The buzzing of nerves inside her disagreed. "I'll look over the rest of the house." Her gaze rested on Sasha. "Stay here." Her dog could keep an eye on Nicolas. Judging by the grin on Sasha's face, she'd fallen in love with him already. *Beat you to it, girl.*

Nicolas took out his cell phone and dialed. He didn't move to follow her, which suited her fine. Given their history, it was best to keep a comfortable distance. She'd feel better if he'd never become involved in the first place. What had Trevor been thinking, asking Nicolas for help after everything Nicolas had lost the last time he'd intervened in a Trevor Swartz created catastrophe? Like a hurricane, her dad brought destruction to anyone in his path.

The ranch house had a long hallway leading off the main living area. Kayla approached the first bedroom. The door already was open, so she peeked inside. It was empty of human presence. Whoever had trashed the house hadn't skipped this room. A purple duffle bag with Olive's name stitched on the front lay askew on the ground near the twin bed. Toys and fluffy stuffed animals filled the space. This was Olive's bedroom.

When Trevor had taken full custody of Olive, he'd gone on a shopping spree. Perhaps to make up for the neglect and abandonment of her mom. Poor child. So much upheaval in Olive's short life heightened Kayla's urgency to find her.

She checked the rest of the bedrooms, careful not to touch anything in order to preserve evidence, before entering the bathroom. The drawers in the cabinet hadn't been disturbed. A large mirror hung over the sink, and Kayla paused to check her reflection. Dark circles hung underneath her eyes. Her body ached after driving hundreds of miles straight through. Once she resolved the issue with her father, she'd head to her mom's house and enjoy some time there before heading home.

A flash of movement behind her in the mirror's reflection caught her attention. The shower curtain slid to the side and someone hurdled out. Kayla's scream was cut off by an arm looping around her throat and squeezing tight. In a panic, she reached behind her to fight back. All she caught was a section of her assailants face mask. She didn't have the leverage to lift it and reveal the person's face. Her oxygen level dropped, and her vision blurred. *I'm not dying in this bathroom.* Using all her strength, she struck out and connected with the person's nose. Her gift of pain offered a small break in Kayla's suffocation. The hold loosened long enough to get out a squeaky cry.

Within a second, the arm constricted again. The feeling of cold metal pressed against her cheek—a knife.

"Give me the necklace and diamonds, or your whole family will die." Her attacker spoke in a gravelly voice.

What necklace? What diamonds? And how was Kayla supposed to tell this person anything when she couldn't breathe?

A bark announced Sasha's arrival. Thank you, God. The dog bounced into the bathroom wearing the golden retriever smile and looking as happy as always. For the first time, Kayla wished Sasha had even a slight killer instinct.

Sasha charged at Kayla and jumped up, setting her front paws on Kayla's chest. The sudden weight pushed

Kayla backward, which caught her attacker by surprise and forced them both off balance. The break was all she needed to free herself from the death grip.

She remembered Nicolas, who she hoped was still in the house, and screamed as loud as her damaged throat could manage.

The person who'd assaulted her jumped away, then bounded through the doorway leading to the main bedroom. Nicolas appeared in the other doorway, which opened to the hall. "Are you okay?"

When she attempted to speak, only a hacking cough sounded. She pointed to the doorway where the intruder had escaped then made a choking gesture. She had never been good at charades.

He stared at her, blinking for several seconds, before darting off toward the bedroom. His shouts soon followed.

Relief flooded her body, and shock turned her muscles into jelly. Kayla lowered herself onto the ground like an abandoned marionette. Trembling like a leaf caught in the wind, she rested her head on the bathroom wall. Whoever had ransacked the house and attacked her had been looking for jewelry and diamonds. What did that have to do with Trevor? How could he be so selfish as to put Olive in danger for jewels? She firmed her resolve to find and protect her sister. First though, she had to catch her breath.

Nicolas chased the home invader until he lost sight of him. The houses in this neighborhood were packed together, providing his target with ample opportunities to dart through backyards and sneak in between houses. Once he realized the chase was fruitless, he paused to catch his breath. Returning, he entered through the sliding glass doors in the main bedroom, then went straight to check on Kayla.

She sat on the floor of the bathroom. Sasha's head rested on her lap. Eyes closed, Kayla inhaled and exhaled in a slow rhythmic beat.

With her guard lowered, he used the moment to catch a good look at her. Her long hair, a beautiful shade of deep brown almost like mahogany, tumbled over her shoulder like water in a mountain stream. She'd added bangs since their high school days, which nicely framed her pretty face. She wore faded jeans and a blue flannel shirt that brought out the color of her eyes. Her hair and casual clothing style suited her.

In high school, his breath had been stolen the moment she introduced herself as his new tutor. Trying to concentrate on homework while Kayla Swartz sat across the table was difficult. He'd done his best though. Nicolas's path in life had been paved with ambitions that didn't include Snowberry, Montana. Since the discovery of his talent for throwing a football, his dad had drilled into him the importance of setting his sights on opportunities not found in his hometown. The world offered fame and fortune for those strong and determined enough to chase it down. He never found fame on the football field but crafted his own success in business. An accomplishment that eventually earned his dad's pride.

He cleared his throat. "I'm sorry. I didn't catch him." He waited for a sign she'd heard him.

With a sharp intake of breath, she opened her eyes. Those beautiful blue orbs stared up at him. "Help me up," she spoke in a scratchy voice.

He took the extended hand and pulled her to her feet. "Are you okay?" His assessing gaze roamed over her body, halting at the streak of red skin around her throat and mouth. Anger swelled.

She nodded. "I'm shaken up but fine. My heart rate is through the roof."

Taking hold of her shaking hand, he brushed a thumb over the smooth surface of her skin. He should have caught the person who attacked her. "Let's get you something to drink, then you can tell me what happened."

Once in the kitchen, he poured a large glass of water and handed it to her, which she downed in under a minute.

Kayla sank into the only remaining upright kitchen chair. "Someone was hiding in the bathtub and tried to strangle me." She coughed, then cleared her throat. "I'm pretty sure it was a woman, judging by the voice. She asked where a necklace and diamonds were. Do you know what she's talking about?"

Nicolas had only recently arrived in Snowberry to spend time with his family over the Easter holiday. He had planned to have coffee with Trevor at some point during his stay, but Trevor canceled their meeting and asked Nicolas come to the house. Fortunately, he was here to help her after the attack. "I wasn't able to get ahold of Trevor. He never mentioned anything about valuable jewels."

"To me neither." Kayla's body slumped. "I'll try calling him one last time. If he's still not answering, then I'll contact the sheriff's department and report the break-in and attack."

The flash of pain in her eyes struck his heart. Everyone in their hometown knew about Trevor's criminal record and all the misdeeds he hadn't been charged with formally. He didn't blame Kayla for holding on to hurt feelings. A year ago, an envelope had arrived at Nicolas's Malibu home. The four-page handwritten letter was from Trevor Swartz, filled with an apology and his commitment to living a better life. After a lifetime of addiction and bad decisions, Trevor had cleaned up. Part of the recovery process was to make amends. Nicolas's injury—an injury he'd sustained while intervening during a bar fight in which Trevor was being beaten senseless—had ended his hopes for a football scholarship. He'd also earned a disorderly conduct charge, adding the one and only mark on his record. Any bad feelings he had about the incident were long passed, and he'd forgiven Trevor, along with providing encouragement on his new path.

Sasha appeared by his leg, peering up with large brown eyes. Weren't humans lucky to have dogs, animals that never seemed to hang on to resentment? He coveted their adaptability.

Kayla removed her cell phone from her coat pocket and checked the screen. "Oh no. I missed a call from Trevor. He called a few minutes ago. I didn't hear it ring." She played the voicemail message on speaker phone.

"Hey, honey, it's me again. I had to leave with Olive before you came. Sorry about that. Look… I can't tell you what's going on over the phone, but please trust me. I need you to come to the Moonlight Motel on Highway 17 to get Olive. I have a few other things that you'll need to take to law enforcement, but just keep them away from our local department." Static sounded. "Honey, whatever you hear about me, don't believe it. You're so smart, and I don't trust anyone else. I'm innocent and I will prove it."

The message ended, and a knot formed in Nicolas's gut. "I called him twice before you yelled for help, and he didn't answer."

She rubbed her temples before placing her phone back into her pocket. Her hands gripped the edge of the table, providing balance for her to stand. "Looks like my road trip isn't over. Come on, Sasha. Let's get back into the car." On the way out of the house, she grabbed the doll that she'd picked up off the living room floor earlier. "Olive's been through a lot. Having a doll to hold on to will provide some comfort."

"Are you sure you're okay to drive? You still seem pretty unsteady." He followed her outside, waging an internal debate. Interfering with other people's troubles did not usually end well for him. Besides his broken throwing arm in high school, while in the army he'd attempted to resolve a fight that resulted in a bullet to his leg and a broken femur. He'd made a rule to mind his own business. As a bodyguard, he fulfilled his professional obligation to the highest level but kept a strict line between personal and business matters. But a little girl might be in danger, and Kayla needed help. Or at least someone watching her back. "I'll go with you." The words left his mouth before he could stop them.

"Thank you, but I feel better now. Or I will feel better once I find Trevor and have Olive safe with me." She held open the door while Sasha hopped into the back seat. "Give me your phone number. I'll call if I need help."

He took her cell phone and saved his number under her contacts. He'd head home now and spend time with his family, which was why he'd returned to Montana in the first place. Running into Kayla, even under these dangerous circumstances, made his trip a lot more interesting. "Promise to call if you need anything. Don't hesitate."

"I will." With a push of a button, she started the engine. "It was nice seeing you again, Nicolas."

As he watched her drive out of sight, his conscience pounded inside his chest. *Don't let her do this alone.* Nicolas glanced at his watch, then back at the street. He should color Easter eggs with his nieces, like he'd planned. That would be the sensible decision.

The memory of Kayla clutching her injured throat in the bathroom jolted him back into reality. He raced to his SUV parked on the street. No one had ever accused him of being sensible.

TWO

Stepping down on the accelerator, Kayla steered the car clear of the curve. The elevation of the road was steadily climbing. Soon, the highway should begin its descent and bring her to her destination. She was accustomed to driving in the mountains, first while growing up in Western Montana and then while living in Colorado. The rolling roads always felt like a well-balanced teeter-totter. Rise then drop then rise then drop, repeating over and over again. Under normal conditions, the sight of red cedars and ponderosa pines along the road breathed life into her soul. But the current churning inside her stomach didn't allow for daydreaming.

Once again, she asked herself what had happened. What had spooked Trevor so deeply he took off before Kayla's arrival? He had something important to hand over to her. Why had he wished to keep it out of the hands of their local law enforcement agency? Someone had threatened her. Threatened her family. She'd respect his wishes for now but not for long. The motel where he'd directed her was located on the outskirts of a small town higher up in the mountains. A more difficult drive than the nearby towns in the valley. He could have left Olive with a neighbor or Kayla's mom. Her parents were on friendly terms. Unless Trevor was worried about Olive's safety. Her analyzing halted when a semitruck carrying a full load of tree trunks buzzed by, heading in the opposite direction. Startled, she reset her attention to the road. Experience had taught her to assume ice was present. Even in early April, the temperatures often dipped below freezing. A light snow had begun falling only a minute ago, dusting the hood of her car and windshield.

Her hands gripped the wheel as she braked for a slow moving vehicle in front of her. *Come on.* The driver wasn't even going the speed limit. Up ahead, the road flattened and ran straight for almost a mile. Kayla waited for an opportunity when oncoming traffic had cleared, then accelerated to pass the slower car before returning to her lane. She couldn't waste time getting to the motel. After she saw Trevor and had Olive, the trip home would go slower and be taken with more care. What if they weren't at the motel when she arrived? The stirring in her gut swelled. *Don't assume the worst.* If someone were after Trevor or something he had, then hiding in an out-of-the-way motel was a decent plan. But Kayla had to get there before anyone else learned where he was. She increased her speed.

A road sign for the motel appeared. Only five more miles. Some of her anxiety eased with the knowledge she'd soon arrive. She activated her windshield wipers. The pavement was wet and tire spray from passing cars created a mess on her windshield. Kayla tapped the button on the steering wheel lever and sent a stream of washer fluid onto the glass. As the windshield wipers swished back and forth to clear her view, she noticed a truck in the oncoming lane speeding down the hillside. The truck raced up to the vehicle ahead of it, then veered into Kayla's lane in order to pass. Seeing the truck heading straight for her car, she panicked. Her heart leaped into her throat. There was no way the truck would clear the other vehicle and return to its own lane in time to prevent a head-on collision.

She pressed down on the horn. The truck stayed its course. Given the larger size of the truck compared to her car, this game of chicken would only end one way— and she'd lose. She thought of Sasha in the back seat.

A safety rail ran along the road to her right, which served as the only barrier between cars and a steep drop-off. Kayla raced to reach the end of the rail and solid ground. She whispered a prayer to God, then jerked the steering wheel to the right. Fighting the urge to close her eyes, she struggled to direct the car forward to a spot clear of rocks and trees. Her car seemed to have a mind of its own, and no matter how strongly she clung to the steering wheel to keep the car moving straight, it swerved toward a large boulder. Using all her strength, she forced the car to swing parallel with the boulder. "Hang tight, Sasha." In a flash, the side of the car collided with the rock. Kayla exhaled in a long rush of breath. The moment the car came to a complete stop, she rotated back to check on Sasha. Her sweet dog panted heavily, appearing scared but unharmed. *Thank you, God, for keeping us safe.*

Now what? Even if her car was drivable, she wouldn't be able to coax it up the embankment and back onto the road. All she could do was call emergency services, then Trevor. He'd have to hold on a little while longer.

She took her phone out of her purse. No service. That wasn't surprising. Cell service around these parts was spotty and often only reliable inside pockets of populated areas. She must not be close enough to the town yet or its cell tower. A knock sounded from the driver's side window. Her heart skipped a beat. At the sight of Nicolas's face looking at her through the glass, she calmed. Thank goodness he'd followed her. The window refused to budge, so she cracked open the car door with a groan—made by both the door and herself.

"Are you all right?" His gaze roamed over her before switching to Sasha in the back seat.

How many times today would he need to ask her that question? "We're fine. At least, I think we are. It's kind of hard to tell since the world hasn't stopped twirling yet." She pressed a hand to her head. Her brain was stuck in the spin cycle.

Nicolas leaned over and peered into her eyes. "Your pupils aren't dilated. Did you hit your head?"

"I don't think so." The quick seconds of the accident had passed in a blur. She strained to remember each moment. "Can you let Sasha out and make sure she's doing okay?"

Without hesitation, he opened the back door. Grabbing onto the dog's leash, he guided her onto the grassy ground.

Sasha's tail wag and bouncy demeanor were enough evidence that she had come through the adventure unharmed.

Kayla took hold of her purse and prepared to leave the car as well. Nicolas grasped her left hand, and she gratefully accepted his assistance. Once Kayla was on her feet, dizziness hit hard. She took a minute to balance, with Nicolas holding on to her around her waist to ensure she didn't tumble off the cliff about a dozen feet behind her. Going against her better judgment, she peaked over at the sharp drop-off and became even woozier. The cloudy gray sky swayed back and forth as if Kayla had stepped onto shore after a month-long sea voyage.

Eventually, the earth grew still under her feet. "I think I can walk now." But where to? The motel? The car accident had delayed her. *Please don't let me be too late.*

"Let's get you and Sasha to my SUV. I was following you when I saw you get run off the road." The muscles in his face hardened. "What was the matter with those people? They could have killed you. They didn't even stop."

"Anyone who drives these roads regularly would never act so reckless." Unless they were racing toward something. Or running away. Kayla shuttered as the sensation of her attacker's grip around her throat returned. "Will you drive me to the motel? I need to get there and warn Trevor." Adrenaline surged. The odds were slim the driver of the truck had any connection to Trevor or his troubles, but the possibility scared her.

"Of course." He held her elbow as they climbed up the slippery ground. His black SUV waited, parked on the shoulder, engine still running.

Kayla let in Sasha, then settled into the passenger seat. The throbbing in her knee did little to distract her from her worry. "Thank you." The words of gratitude cracked with her overwhelming emotion. Now, to get Olive and whatever Trevor had to hand over. Given Nicolas was injured the last time he attempted to help her, she prayed she wasn't leading him into another dangerous situation.

"What about your car?" From his perch in the driver's seat, Nicolas peered at the crumpled vehicle. They'd been gifted a miracle. He'd witnessed the incident, which seemed to have had happened in slow motion. In the nausea-inducing moments as the truck sped directly toward Kayla's car, he'd felt helpless. All he could do was watch and pray the truck would move out of the way before impact.

Instead, Kayla had made it past the safety railing and swerved off the road. The front passenger side had taken the brunt of the crash, and the wheel axle was twisted. He gazed over at her and once again was amazed at her grit. She'd almost died, and her immediate thoughts were to get to her dad and help her little sister.

"My car?" She gazed down at the metal shape

pressed up against the boulder. "Leave it for now. It's not going anywhere. I'll call a tow truck after I reach the motel and talk to Trevor."

He nodded and checked for an opening in traffic, then pulled back onto the highway. When he noticed her shiver, he turned up the heat. "You'd make a good race car driver. I had a hard time keeping up with you."

A slow grin spread across her face. "You sound like my mom. If I'd known you were following me, I may have taken it easy."

"I haven't driven in the mountains around this area much since leaving home. It's a different feel than maneuvering through Los Angeles traffic." He'd grown soft living in sunny Southern California during the past five years. While he was in the military, he experienced various climates and conditions. He'd loved outdoor winter activities while growing up in Montana. A person couldn't be a product of this rugged land and cower from icy winds and feet of snow.

"You live in California?" Kayla's eyebrow rose in question. "That is definitely unlike Snowberry."

"It's a different world. I run a bodyguard service for celebrities and other wealthy people, and LA is where the clients are." Up ahead, the sign appeared for the Moonlight Motel. Relief rushed in. They could find Trevor, then make the return trip home, without further incident, he hoped. He'd return Kayla to her mom's house and get back to his family. Their time together would come to an end, something he should want. Remembrances of his teenage crush on Kayla Swartz seemed unavoidable when he was with her. Almost absentmindedly, he touched the bracelet on his left wrist, his favorite colors handwoven in its threads. Kayla had made it for him at the end of their junior year, and he rarely had taken it off since.

Both of Kayla's eyebrows arched. "A bodyguard? Interesting. Sometime you'll have to tell me all about the lifestyles of the rich and famous."

He eased on the brake to turn into the motel parking lot. "I tag along to the glamour events but happily stay on the perimeter. After some of the things I've witnessed on the job, I avoid those types of scenes in my personal life." The quick high of a fun time often led to long-lasting regret. Too often, he'd seen guilt and remorse etched on the faces of his clients.

"I don't even want to imagine what goes on during a Hollywood party. There's Trevor's truck." Kayla pointed to a blue pickup truck that had equal amounts of rust and paint. "I assume he's in one of the rooms nearby."

Several people were situated on the sidewalk that ran alongside the front of the motel. They clustered together, and one appeared to be crying.

Nicolas zipped into an open parking spot.

Before he cut the engine, Kayla hopped out. "What's going on?" She directed the question at the group.

He wasted no time and followed her over to the sidewalk. *I have a bad feeling about this.*

The sobbing woman wiped at her tear-streaked face. She pointed to the door cracked open. "There's been a murder."

* * *

Please, let Olive be all right. Her concern for Trevor was eclipsed by her fear that Olive had been harmed. An innocent little girl shouldn't pay the price for a grown man's mistakes. "I need to see."

Nicolas placed a hand on her shoulder. "Why not wait until the sheriff's department arrives?"

A stout man wearing denim jeans, a heavy canvas jacket and a cowboy hat blew his red-tipped nose into a tissue. "About ten minutes ago, I was working at the front desk when I heard gunshots. Then I ran outside and saw a dark truck driving off, tires squealing. The door had been left open to this room here, so I checked inside and saw a man lying on the floor, bleeding. I called 911 as soon as I knew someone had been shot dead. The nearest deputy is fifteen miles away. No knowing when they'll get here."

Shot dead. The phrase struck hard. "Has anyone seen a little girl about three years old?" Her voice was tinged with fear and desperation.

The small assembly of bystanders all shook their heads.

"I have to find out if Trevor's been shot. If so, I need to find Olive." She glanced up at Nicolas. His attention was focused on the motel room door. A muscle in his jaw twitched and his eyes narrowed. Towering over everyone else at well over six feet, he no doubt made an efficient bodyguard. Kayla had never needed a bodyguard until now. Her life had never been in danger until earlier today. Having Nicolas at her side wrapped her in a layer of comfort.

"I'll go in with you," he said. "If we're entering a crime scene, we'll both need to be very careful."

Kayla closed her eyes and breathed deeply. Her relationship with her father had never been good. He'd brought disappointment and shame into her otherwise peaceful life. During her early teen years, she'd wanted a second chance at a real father-daughter relationship. She dropped by for visits and invited him to work together on her seventh grade science project. She held the assumption that if she were an entertaining daughter, she'd keep Trevor's interest. If Kayla tried hard, did better, acted more fun, Trevor would choose spending time with her over all the other people and places that stole his attention. Looking back, she blamed her naivete on her faith that he was capable of change. So many years wasted craving the impossible.

Despite her history with Trevor, she didn't wish him dead. He could be in another room with Olive.

A brass room number was affixed to the door: 6. *Please don't let Trevor be inside.* Using the toe of her boot, Kayla pushed in the door. The smell of mildew and sulfur hit her. Upon an initial view, she observed a green stained carpet, two beds that filled up most of the space and an old TV set on a crooked dresser, but no dead body in sight.

"He's sprawled out on the floor between the beds," the man wearing a cowboy hat said from behind. "You'll need to go in farther."

"I can check it out. I know what Trevor looks like." Nicolas moved inside the room. "Stay out here."

She was ready to agree when she caught sight of a pile of little girl's clothing. "Olive," she shouted. "Olive, are you here?" Kayla rushed in, past Nicolas. "I have to find her."

He appeared at her side. "We will find her. Let me check the man on the ground." A few long strides brought him to the foot of one of the beds. He glanced down and rubbed the back of his neck.

In that instant, she knew the opportunity to make amends with her father had ended. She swayed on her feet. *I have to see for myself.* Kayla stepped with care. Once next to Nicolas, she viewed his body. Her vision blurred with tears. Even a man like Trevor didn't deserve to die like this.

He'd taken three bullets to his torso. Trevor lay on his stomach with his face turned to the side. Blood pooled around his upper body—a crimson embrace.

"I'm sorry I didn't get here sooner." One tear slid down her cheek. Regret mixed with grief.

"If you'd been here, you would have been hurt too." Nicolas stroked her back.

"Or killed." She swallowed the lump in her throat. If Olive had been in the motel room, had she been hurt? Been taken? If Trevor's murderer was searching for valuable jewelry, then what use was a little girl? Kayla stepped forward and away from Nicolas's soothing touch. His concern was comforting. She couldn't allow distraction. Not with her father dead and her sister missing. Olive might also be in the crosshairs of a murderer.

She gathered her nerve and went about searching the room, cautious not to step on or touch anything. Inside the bathroom, things appeared normal. The towels were crisply folded and the tiny shampoo and soap lined neatly on the counter. "The motel room hasn't been tossed like his house," she said when exiting the bathroom. Aside from the clothing, she saw no signs of Olive.

"Olive, it's your sister, Kayla. If you're here, please let me know. I'm here to help." The bedside lamp had been knocked over and the bedding appeared in disarray. Trevor may have struggled with the shooter prior to his murder.

Kneeling, Nicolas lowered himself to the floor, peered beneath the bed skirt, straightened, then stood. "She's not hiding under the bed."

Her heart sank. How could she find the little girl when she had no idea who'd shot Trevor? Who had he crossed? She worked to bring forward the memory of the near-miss car crash. The driver had been a man. Her attacker at Trevor's house had been a woman. The scent of blood turned her stomach. "I need some air."

Outside, she placed her hands on her knees and hunched over, taking slow, purposeful breaths. Anxiety wrapped around her like a rope, squeezing tight. The whine of sirens drifted in the air. Law enforcement would arrive soon. Would they make finding Olive a top priority?

Nicolas joined her outside the room. "I hear something." He cocked his head. "Listen. Do you hear crying?"

Kayla strained to pick up the noise. The only sounds

she identified were sirens and chatter of the nearby group of people. Then a faint cry hit her. "Where is it coming from?" At the busy motel, another child could be crying. Yet hope sprung. Olive could still be nearby somewhere. She had to be. The other option was too horrible to contemplate.

THREE

Not wasting another moment, Kayla charged back into the motel room with Nicolas hot on her heels. The crying had hushed, and she stood beside the foot of the bed straining to hear any noise coming from nearby. She avoided the sight of her father lying dead on the floor only feet away and suppressed her urge to flee the scene until she was far, far away.

"There's a rustling coming from the closet." Nicolas pointed to the closed accordion door placed at the rear of the room.

Please let Olive be inside unharmed. The crying she'd heard while standing outside resumed. "She's in there. Let me open the door. You may scare her."

He nodded. "I don't exactly look like a cuddly teddy bear."

True. Nicolas had a solid build, being a former soldier and current bodyguard. "Can you get Sasha from your SUV? She *is* a cuddly ball of fluff." Kayla tiptoed over to the closet door. Using the cuff of her coat sleeve to cover her hand, she grabbed the handle and slid it open. Her breath caught in her throat.

A tiny girl sat curled in a tight ball in the far corner of the dark space. Tears streaked her pink cheeks. Her hands clutched a pastel purple stuffed bunny. She stared up at Kayla with wide blue eyes—the color matched her own.

"Olive," Kayla said while lowering to the floor. "Do you remember me? I'm Kayla, your sister." They'd only met twice, the last time at Christmas. She crossed her legs and relaxed her body. The child appeared scared but unharmed. "Did Daddy tell you that I was coming for you?"

Olive swallowed hard. She didn't speak.

"You're safe now with me." Pausing, Kayla considered her approach—gentle and firm. She couldn't push the child but had to build trust. A tall order when they were located in the same room where their father had been shot to death. "What's the name of your bunny?"

Her arms trembled as they pulled the stuffed animal closer to her body. "Hoppy. Papa gave it to me. Where's Papa?"

The inquiry triggered a sharp pain around her heart. How to explain this all to a three-year-old? Olive had been abandoned by her mom, and her other parent had been murdered. "Papa had to leave. Can I pick up you and Hoppy and carry you outside? I have a special friend I'd like you to meet."

In a swift move, Olive stretched out her arms toward Kayla.

She scooped up the girl and prayed for guidance. Her work as a high school teacher and therapy dog handler hadn't fully prepared her for being responsible for a traumatized child. "Put your head down on my shoulder, sweetie, and don't look up or open your eyes until I say so, okay?"

Once Olive squeezed her eyes shut and rested her forehead on Kayla's shoulder, Kayla stood. She hustled out of the room, then took welcome breaths of fresh air. "You can open your eyes now."

"Puppy," Olive squealed, pointing to Sasha.

Nicolas held Sasha's leash. A smile calmed the tension on his face. "Do you want to pet the puppy?"

Olive's answer was to wiggle out of Kayla's arms. Once her feet touched the ground, she beelined for the dog.

"I'll keep an eye on them," Nicolas said. "The sheriff's deputy just arrived."

Her gaze traveled from Nicolas to the deputy exiting the sheriff's department truck. She wanted answers. "Thank you," she whispered to Nicolas. His presence left her with a mix of discomfort and reassurance. She did not want him hurt again while trying to help her with a family problem, but she couldn't summon the will to send him away. Not when threats swirled around them.

Kayla knelt down before her sister. "My friend Nicolas is going to stay with you and the puppy. I'll be close and come back soon."

After a quick nod, Olive's attention returned to the dog, and Sasha went to work—providing comfort and distraction.

Kayla marched over to where the plainclothes deputy stood assessing the scene. She read her badge and recognized the name. "Deputy Reimer. I'm Kayla Swartz. I don't know if you remember me from high school. The shooting victim was my father, Trevor Swartz." The reality of his violent death had started sinking in. With the activity around her stilled, she'd found herself suspended under the weight of emotions.

"Yes, Kayla, I remember you." Christina Reimer held out a hand for a handshake. "It's Detective Reimer but call me Christina. My condolences. Several deputies are en route along with Sheriff Gomez. Any idea what happened?"

"I wish I knew." A whirlwind of sensations formed inside her. She grieved the loss of a man she didn't like, who'd negatively affected her life, but still was her blood. "Trevor asked me to come home to Snowberry to get my half sister, Olive." Kayla pointed to the girl whose arms were wrapped around Sasha. The sight calmed some of her anxiety. "He'd said he was in trouble and needed my help. When I got to his house, he and Olive were gone and the house was tossed. While I was there, someone attacked me. The person sounded female and demanded I give her a necklace and diamonds."

Detective Reimer's head jerked up. She fixed her attention on Kayla instead of her notepad. "A valuable necklace and about two dozen uncut diamonds were recently stolen. Did you find them at your dad's house?"

"No." Her father lived a modest life and committed simple crimes. The idea that he'd steal jewelry and diamonds didn't fit with the man she knew. "We didn't stay long enough to get a good look around. I received a voicemail from Trevor, asking me to meet him here to get Olive. I left right away." She omitted the part about the items Trevor had wanted to give her. Perhaps the much sought after necklace and diamonds? Handing them over to Kayla to turn in to law enforcement didn't make sense though.

"You said *we*. Who was with you?" Detective Reimer asked.

"Nicolas Galanis." Kayla felt her face grow warm. *Get a grip. You're not in high school anymore.* After Nicolas was injured trying to break up a bar fight involving her dad, the news had flown through school with supersonic speed. The football team never made it to the playoffs, and Kayla sat at the center of blame. If Nicolas hadn't been involved with her, he would have finished a championship football season. She was demoted in social status from bookish art nerd to someone no one wanted to be seen with, and she spent most of her senior year in the library when she wasn't in class. As for Nicolas, his senior year ended under a cloud of physical recovery and legal issues. Eventually, the charges against him were dropped, and he had no issue enlisting in the army.

"Hmm." Lips pressed together, Detective Reimer cast a glance at Nicolas, who was standing on the motel walkway next to Olive and Sasha. "I need to secure the crime scene and interview the people who were here at the time of the shooting." Her gaze returned to Kayla before she reached over to give her a brief hug. "I'm sorry about your loss and that we're seeing each other again under these circumstances. Can you meet me over at Trevor's house later for an interview and walk-through? That scene will be processed as well."

"Sure." Kayla stuffed her hands in her jacket pockets. She and Christina hadn't been friends in high school, but a thread of trust connected them now. The severe judgment she'd suffered from being Trevor Swartz's daughter might no longer carry the same weight. At least not with some people. Nicolas appeared willing to put their past behind them. A second chance. Not at romance. Only the assurance he no longer detested her would be enough. "Call me when you are heading over, and I'll join you." She recited her cell phone number. "I'll take Olive to my mom's house, which is where I'm staying while in Snowberry."

Christina's lips pressed into a thin line. "Trevor was Olive's father. Who is her mother? Are you her only next of kin?"

"Trevor had sole custody," Kayla explained. "Olive's mom had some issues and signed away her parental rights. As far as I know, I'm the only family Olive has." Later, Kayla would consider what that meant for her own life. Changes were coming. She had no intention of letting her sister be taken in by the system.

"I'll contact social services and forward your information. Take Olive to your mom's. She'll be safe and well cared for there." Detective Reimer adjusted the brim of her baseball cap, which had *Temple County Sheriff's Department* stitched over the front with red lettering.

A cool wind whipped from the north, biting at the bare skin on her face. Kayla had forgotten how tight a grip winter held on to Montana, only acquiescing when the sun's influence grew too strong. Her spring break vacation ended in five days, and she'd likely be required to remain in Snowberry for a while longer. *Take on one problem and one day at a time.* She'd bring Olive to her mom's house and get settled.

Detective Reimer lifted her ringing cell phone, but before she answered the call, she caught Kayla's gaze. "If you do find the necklace and diamonds or hear anything about them, call me right away." She handed over a business card. "Right away." The two words spoken with firm clarity. "I'll request a patrol car drive by your mom's house every hour or so. Let us know if you see anything or anyone suspicious."

The urgency in her voice couldn't be missed. Murder in these parts was rare. Kayla hadn't lived in this region for fifteen years, but the general sense of safety hadn't changed. Trevor had made enemies along the criminal path he'd chosen to travel. Had someone finally gotten revenge? Her gut told her that after her father's desperate pleas for help and his murder, something more complicated was simmering underneath the surface.

Right now, her focus turned to Olive. Considering the view of Nicolas, Olive and Sasha, she took a moment to appreciate the vignette. A lot of puzzle pieces had to be put into place in the next few days. Law enforcement would protect Kayla and Olive, and soon, she hoped, find the killer. The end of Nicolas's involvement was unsettling, but he had his own family obligations. An ache settled in her chest as she anticipated saying goodbye to him.

* * *

While removing the car seat from Trevor's unlocked truck, Nicolas dammed up his sorrow. He'd only begun to understand Trevor, a man who'd lived a complicated life. Trevor's impact on Kayla and, to lesser extent, himself couldn't be minimized. But the man had worked to change. To be better. But as of tonight, he would never have the chance to make amends to his oldest daughter.

Nicolas shut the door of the truck, then carried the car seat over to his SUV. "I have no idea how these things work," he pleaded to Kayla.

"Neither do I." She stood watch over Olive and Sasha. The little girl stroked the dog's fur with one hand and clutched her stuffed bunny with the other.

"How hard can it be?" His question captured the attention of a nearby motel guest.

"Let me get that in for you," a middle-aged man in sweatpants and a Montana State hoodie said. "I have five kids, which makes me a certified car seat expert."

"Thanks." Nicolas handed over the car seat and opened the back door of his SUV. He watched as the man worked with quick efficiency.

"All set." Montana State hoodie man glanced at his handiwork and grinned. "Make sure the straps on the car seat are secure over the child's body." He stuffed his hands into the front pocket of his hoodie. "I'm sorry about your loss. Seeing such a tragedy is a reminder we need to watch out for one another. Lend a hand when we can."

"Appreciate the help." Nicolas shook the man's hand. "Kayla, are you okay to leave?"

She glanced at the open door of the motel room. Crime scene tape was up, allowing no one inside but law enforcement. Would they find the person or people responsible for murdering Trevor? What about Olive? Had the murderer known she was inside the room as a possible witness? His urgency to move Kayla and Olive far away from here increased.

"Let's go." She reached for Olive and scooped her up in her arms. "Come, Sasha. Time for another car ride."

Once everyone was inside the vehicle, Nicolas looked in the rearview mirror. Sasha was snuggled next to Olive, who was secure in her car seat. "She's an amazing dog."

The corners of Kayla's mouth lifted. "She's a trained therapy dog. We volunteer part time at the hospital, mostly working in the children's wing. Sasha has the instinct to seek out those who need comfort and then stay with them until their anxiety eases. She senses Olive's distress. I'm glad I have her along."

"Your sister has been through a lot recently." He turned onto the highway that led to Snowberry. The memory of what was left behind, lying on the bloody carpet, clogged his throat. Trevor was with God. He was at peace. Those left on earth would experience heartache and grief. Though not many people would mourn Trevor Swartz, Nicolas resolved to honor the man. He'd keep Kayla and Olive safe, and help find those responsible for Trevor's murder.

Kayla glanced over her shoulder and sighed. "I don't know how to take care of a toddler."

"You'll figure it out. Your mom will be there to help."

He'd only met Kayla's mom once; on the night he'd gone to her house to pick up Kayla for their first date. His nerves had been buzzing that entire day, and when he'd marched up the stairs to the front door, his stomach had almost emptied over the rose bushes by the patio. He had wanted their time together to be perfect. It had taken him months to work up the nerve to ask her out. Once his blinders came off in their tutoring sessions and he'd seen her beauty as well as her smarts and wit, he'd wanted to be more than her tutoring student.

His dreams had been filled with Kayla, but those dreams had morphed into a nightmare the evening he'd been taken to the hospital with an injury that ended his football career. Kayla, through no fault of her own, became the scapegoat for the team's disappointing season and Nicolas's anger. They'd never spoke again, until today. Still ashamed of his behavior, especially toward Kayla, he vowed to make amends. Instead of caring about Kayla after his injury, he'd shown the opposite of love. He could have been blessed with her in his life for all these years instead of being a stranger. If they could reestablish their friendship, he'd leave for California content.

Nicolas prayed that Trevor's troubles didn't end in injury to Kayla or Olive—or even worse—another death.

FOUR

The moment the vehicle pulled into the driveway, Kayla's mom rushed out of the front door. Tears streaked her cheeks.

The sight produced tears in Kayla's eyes, and she was unable to hold back any longer. They'd be safe here, she and Olive. Kayla could refocus and regroup before heading to Trevor's house to talk with Detective Reimer. She hopped out of the SUV and found herself wrapped in her mom's embrace. "Hey, Mom. I'm fine. Olive is fine."

Her mom, Hillary, squeezed Kayla even harder. "I'm so sorry about Trevor, honey. I'm so sorry." She kissed Kayla's cheek before letting go. Her gaze moved to the back seat and the little girl. "I offered a prayer of thanksgiving to God when you texted me that you had Olive."

"I found her hiding in the closet of the motel room Trevor had been shot in." Kayla took a sharp inhale of breath, imagining the terror Olive must have felt. "Sasha has been by her side ever since. I hope she knows she's safe."

"I'm sure she does." Her mom brushed a hand across her hair before turning to Nicolas.

He had exited the SUV and was releasing Olive from her car seat. Within seconds, the little girl was in his arms.

Kayla's heart stuttered at the sight of him looking completely natural holding a child. Nicolas possessed strength and gentleness. Why he'd established a relationship with Trevor, which had resulted in him being at the house when Kayla arrived, remained a mystery. She was grateful for whatever forces had brought them together. But now he'd return to his parents' house, then soon to Los Angeles. For their security, she wished he would stay, but she refused to ask more of him than he'd already given.

She held out her hands to accept Olive. "I'll take her. I'm sure your family is worried."

"I make a living putting myself in harm's way. They're always worried about me." His grin displayed wry humor. "I should probably go put my mom's mind at ease. I'm sure the news has spread around town. I'll come back if you need anything. Even just someone to talk to."

"I appreciate the offer." Her father had been the main supply of town gossip for decades. Snowberry and the surrounding area would need to find another source of drama to fill the void. Her ties to Trevor drove her away from Snowberry. Kayla had hated the stares of the townspeople and could almost read their minds. Trevor Swartz's daughter had to be no good, like the man himself.

Kayla had worked hard in school to prove otherwise. But facts didn't matter when rumors tasted sweeter. And then, when Nicolas was injured trying to protect Kayla and Trevor, all hope of redeeming herself was lost.

Her face grew warm as she took in the sight of Nicolas's handsome face. The soft heartbeat of their youthful connection remained. She couldn't allow it to strengthen. Not when she couldn't trust her emotions, especially now. "Thanks for everything you've done though. I'm so glad you followed me to the motel."

"I'm not good at following instructions." Another charismatic grin. "I'm staying in Snowberry for a few more days. I can be over in minutes if needed. Law enforcement will find those responsible."

"Knowing Trevor, I'm sure the list of suspects is long." Kayla held Olive tighter. "Thanks again." Not able to bear a prolonged goodbye, she turned on her heels and carried Olive into her mom's house with Sasha following. She stood at the front room window and watched the dark SUV back out of the driveway until it disappeared down the road. Her body emptied like someone had opened a tap and all her energy had flowed out. She sank into the sofa and set Olive beside her. "You're safe now with me and Ms. Hillary. We'll take care of you."

"I'm hungry," Olive declared, then popped her thumb in her mouth.

"Kayla, you look spent." Her mom's observations were correct, as usual. "I'll bring Olive into the kitchen to fix her something to eat. Go take a moment to catch your breath. You've been tested today. Take as much time as you need. Sasha and I will watch Olive until you feel steady on your feet again."

"You're the best." How Trevor had snared a saint like her mom was beyond Kayla's comprehension. They stayed together long enough to have Kayla, then her mom left the relationship with her daughter.

With Olive now tucked in the kitchen with her mom likely serving her cookies and milk—the go-to comfort snack in this house—Kayla let her head fall back, resting on the sofa cushion. Behind her closed eyes, she saw her father's body. Had he been killed for stolen jewels? Trevor hadn't been a good father to Kayla growing up, but he never put her in direct danger. At least not that she could remember. Soon, sleep wrapped her in a soft blanket. Her mind drifted to Nicolas and the feelings of security his unexpected company had brought. Their friendship had been built during hours together in tutoring sessions. She'd been sure her crush went unreciprocated until the day Nicolas had asked her out. Her feet had walked on clouds for the rest of the week. Why did the cutest guy in school want to date her, a nobody? He'd made her feel like somebody though. Someone special, at least to him.

A crash startled her awake. Her mind and body assumed danger. She jumped off the sofa and groggily rushed to the kitchen. Finding her mom standing over a pile of shattered glass on the floor, Kayla's heart slowed. "Are you okay?"

"Clumsy me. I was drying a drinking glass and dropped it." Her mom shook her head. "My nerves haven't been this rattled since the first time I took you out driving."

"Oh my." Laughing, she grabbed the broom and dustpan from the hall closet. Before returning to the kitchen, she glanced out the front window. The sight of a patrol car moving along the street at a slow speed reassured her. She'd prefer round-the-clock surveillance, but a rural county sheriff department's resources only stretched so far. "That's a high standard for rattled nerves. You almost had a nervous breakdown teaching me to drive."

Kayla's mom tossed the dish towel over her shoulder. "I can't imagine how you're feeling. Olive is sleeping in your old room with Sasha. Sit down and I'll make you a cup of tea. Do you want peanut butter or chocolate chip cookies?"

"Both, please. It has been a day." Once the broken glass was deposited in a paper bag and put into the trash, Kayla sat at the table. "Do you have any idea what's going on?" While Kayla distanced herself from Snowberry and her father, her mom remained a lifelong citizen. She worked and volunteered in the community. She'd also kept the lines of communication open with Trevor. Her mom's large heart held space for anyone in need, including her ex-husband.

"Let me get the tea ready, and then we can talk." As the water came up to temperature in the kettle on the stove, her mom spooned loose leaf tea in two strainers, then placed them inside ceramic cups. The kettle whistled. She filled each cup with steaming water and carried them to the table, setting one before Kayla.

The scents of orange and mint filled Kayla's nose—
a welcome reminder she was home. She grabbed another cookie, chocolate chip this time, and sank her
teeth into it.

Kayla's mom took a sip of tea; her gaze fixed on her.
"I have no idea what Trevor might have gotten mixed
up in. You know he went to rehab a few years ago,
after Olive was born. He was a changed man afterward.
When you came up last fall to visit, you saw how different he was. He wanted to be a good dad to Olive and
to you, albeit belatedly. He was in the process of making amends."

"The last time I saw him, I didn't believe he really
transformed into a new and improved man. At least not
permanently." There'd been missed calls from Trevor
that went ignored. When she'd received a card in the
mail from him for her last birthday, she tossed it un-
opened in the trash. Words of apology and love meant
nothing without actions to back them up. Growing up,
she'd believed his excuses and promises to do better
until she accepted Trevor would never change. Kayla's
jar of forgiveness had run dry.

"I think you would have seen the differences for
yourself if you'd been able to spend more time with
him and Olive." Her mom dabbed at the corners of her
eyes with a tissue.

Kayla let the statements sink in. Her opportunity
to spend more time with him had been severed. Had
Trevor really made a good-faith effort to change, or was
he pulling another deception? Nicolas offered forgiveness to the man who'd been responsible for the end of

his dreams of a football championship and scholarship. Why? She wished she'd had the chance to get more information from Nicolas about what had triggered his change of heart.

"I have Olive to consider." Her worry shifted to the little girl sleeping down the hall. "Trevor told me during my last visit that he listed me as her guardian in his will. I didn't think much about it at the time." Though she should have. "Moving her to Colorado Springs right away isn't a good idea." Had the threat dissipated with Trevor's death? Or redirected to them?

With a sniffle, her mom took a cookie from off the plate. "I agree. What's your plan?"

"My first order of business is to protect Olive by ensuring the sheriff's department catches Trevor's murderer. Besides that, I'll contact social services and a lawyer." She sipped her tea. A counselor for both of them would be a good idea too. "I'll need to make arrangements for Trevor." Her heart rate increased.

Guardianship and burial arrangements were things she hadn't planned on worrying about during her visit. Add a car repair to the list. Kayla would call a towing company and have her car brought to a local repair shop. Her suitcase and Sasha's things were still inside the vehicle. She'd take a trip to the store today to get dog food, although Sasha would be content eating people food until Kayla retrieved their belongings.

"I'll help with whatever is needed," her mom said. "You mattered so much to your dad. He'd wanted to get his second chance with you right."

"Instead, he was shot dead." The sharp pain of grief took another stab. "Whether he was trying to clean up his life or not, Trevor got into trouble, and that trouble got him killed."

"You don't know that for sure," her mom said in a hushed voice. "Don't make a judgment until you learn the entire story."

"You're too trusting." Kayla pushed to her feet and started pacing. Her earlier exhaustion had turned into caged energy.

"And you've hardened your heart." Standing as well, Kayla's mom placed herself in her path and extended her hands. She pulled Kayla into a hug, absorbing some of her distress. "Focus on Olive. She needs stability and security right now. She needs you."

"I just went from single dog mom to raising my half sister." As a child, every birthday wish had been for a sibling. When Olive had come to live with Trevor, Kayla had attempted to connect with her. Unfortunately, her hard feelings about Trevor had gotten in the way. "I will need your help."

"Of course, honey. You know I'm here for whatever you and Olive need." Her mom returned to her kitchen chair and cradled the cup of tea in her hands. "Are you ever going to tell me what Nicolas Galanis was doing with you?"

Kayla knew this question was coming, which didn't lessen the blush on her face. Instantly, she was transformed from grieving daughter into a teenager denying a crush. "Nicolas was at Trevor's house when I arrived.

Trevor had asked him to come over." She left out the part about her attack in the bathroom, then being run off the road. No need to send her mom into a panic after the fact. "He helped find Olive at the motel."

"If he's been so helpful, why send him home?" her mom asked. "I have enough cookies to share with him too."

Kayla chuckled. "You always have enough cookies around the house to pass around to the entire town. Nicolas is better off far away from me. Especially right now." Again, she didn't mention the attack on her or the stolen diamonds and a necklace. Kayla would remain vigilant. She had to shield Olive and her mom from danger. "We don't need a repeat of the past."

"The way Nicolas looked at you a little while ago while standing in my driveway, I believe he'd rather be close to you."

She opened her mouth to issue her dispute, but a scream coming from the direction of the bedrooms stilled her. Her blood froze. Another scream followed, this one louder. Kayla raced out of the kitchen and down the hallway. Had someone broken in to silence a witness? Judging from Olive's screams, she wouldn't be quieted without a fight. And whomever threatened Olive had to deal with Kayla too.

Sasha's barking hushed as Kayla burst into the bedroom.

She quickly scanned the room. It was empty of intruders. She rushed over to the bed and knelt beside it. "Olive, what's wrong? Are you hurt?"

The girl clutched her stuffed bunny to her chest. "Bad man get me."

She climbed on the bed and pulled Olive onto her lap. "No one will get you. Sasha is here to keep you safe. So am I and Ms. Hillary. No one is going to hurt you, baby. I promise." A hurricane of sorrow and anger blustered inside her. Adults made mistakes, and often innocent children paid the price. "You had a bad dream, that's all."

Tears spilled out of Olive's eyes and flowed down her ruby red cheeks. "Papa."

Kayla's heart ached. "Papa isn't here right now. Would you like me to read you a story?" Books had helped her escape from reality. Still did. She went over to the bookshelf in her room that held a few of her favorite childhood stories. After a brief search, she found one, then snuggled in bed with Olive.

Sasha tucked herself at the end of the bed by their feet.

While Kayla read, she remained alert for signs of an approaching threat.

Olive's body eventually slackened against her.

She tucked her sister under the covers, gave Sasha instructions to stay, and tiptoed out of the bedroom. Olive's bad dream had rattled both of them. Thankfully, Olive had been able to relax back into sleep. Kayla, on the other hand, stayed fixed on the memories of her attack in the bathroom. Delayed reaction to trauma, perhaps. More likely, it was her brain's way of reminding her that the boogeyman was real. They'd killed Trevor. Might have killed Kayla if Sasha hadn't charged to the rescue. She thought about calling Nicolas but stopped the idea from lingering. Kayla might not be former military or a trained bodyguard, but she had a burning desire to protect her family. She'd do anything to keep Olive safe, including the possibility of reaching out to her old flame.

FIVE

The next morning, Nicolas poured a cup of coffee and fought the urge to drive to Hillary's house to check on Kayla and Olive. They'd been on his mind all night. Around dinnertime yesterday, Detective Reimer had called to ask him to stop by Trevor's house in the morning to provide a statement. He'd agreed, wishing to see Kayla again and wanting to help. Worry had his gut tied up in knots.

"Morning." He greeted his sister, Emma, as she entered the kitchen. "You want coffee?"

"Yes," she said with a yawn. "I got up before the kids so I could enjoy a few moments of quiet and watch the sun come up." Emma was a year younger than him and was the sibling who knew him best. They were a lot alike in demeanor. Though, while Nicolas had carried the weight of expectation during his youth, Emma had been free to decide her own life.

Their father, or Pops as he was called in the Galanis house, had a soft spot for his daughters. Contrasted with the firm hand he used on his only son, Nicolas. Elias Galanis had emigrated from Greece as a child, moved to Montana as a young man and married. Nicolas's parents had a happy marriage, but he sensed a restlessness in his pops. He wondered if Pops hadn't settled down and had a family at a young age, he might have pursued his own dreams. Instead, he placed them squarely on Nicolas's shoulders with the expectation that his son would fulfill them.

Nicolas poured Emma a mug of coffee, then slipped on his boots and coat. They both went outside, bundled up to protect against the chilly morning air.

Steam billowed off the surface of his coffee as he took a drink. Leaning on the porch railing, he breathed deeply. The sun was appearing over the mountain in the distance, casting the snowcapped peak in sparkling light.

Emma gave him a sideward glance. "Do you think getting mixed up with Kayla Swartz is a smart idea? Mom and Pops weren't happy you were with her yesterday, especially after they heard Trevor Swartz had been murdered."

He considered his family's point of view. They all thought of Kayla as a nice girl with a troubled father. But no one wanted a repeat of his injury senior year of high school. "I can take care of myself. Don't worry. Remember, I'm skilled at getting hurt anywhere, not only with Kayla."

She snorted a laugh. "True. Mom and Pops are worried you'll get into trouble with the law again. Criminal charges could affect your business. And if I had to guess, they're concerned about your feelings for Kayla too."

Interesting observation. "I owe Kayla my friendship. Helping her is the least I can do after how I treated her senior year." His chest burned with shame. He should have done better by her. "And I won't get in trouble with the law. I'm assisting the sheriff's department this time, not jumping into the fray."

"I get it." Emma's gaze wandered over the backyard. A large barn was set back from the house. Inside, about a dozen horses waited for their morning meal and then to be let out into the pasture. "I liked Kayla in school. I'm sure she's still really nice. You two were cute together when you dated. But you know how Pops is."

He knew all too well. *Don't let falling for a girl get in the way of achieving your goals. You have a chance to make it big, to make a name for yourself. Keep focused on what's important.* His pops's words rang in his head. Being raised with the pressure to always win made shaking that mindset difficult. Nicolas was no longer a teenager with stars in his eyes. He hadn't played professional football but had made a name for himself in another way. A successful business with wealthy clients held as much merit in Pops's eyes.

"I'm working on being okay without Pops's approval." He inhaled deeply. "Don't tell him that."

"Never." Emma grinned. "I always have your back." She sighed. "Are you joining us for egg dyeing today? Your nieces didn't want to dye them yesterday because they were afraid you'd feel left out."

He chuckled, then downed the rest of his coffee. "I should be back after I talk to Detective Reimer. I'd hate to miss out." Nicolas went back into the house, took a shower and dressed. After he was done at Trevor's house and before Easter egg dyeing, he'd call his business partner to touch base. They'd signed a large contract last week, and preparation was key to providing the service level that validated their fees.

As he passed through the kitchen, his progress halted at the sight of his mom.

"Where are you going?" his mom asked from her spot by the stove. She set down the spatula and turned to him, folding her arms. "You didn't eat breakfast."

"Sorry, Mom. I'll eat when I get back. Promise." He crossed his heart and kissed his mom on the cheek. "The sheriff's department wants to talk to me about what happened yesterday."

She tsked. "You be careful, son. There's rumors around town about the things Trevor's buddies were into. They're mixed up with some bad people."

"I don't think Trevor was." How could Nicolas be certain? He based his opinion of Trevor off recent communications, but Nicolas hadn't been around Snowberry to see for himself. "I'll be fine. I make a living watching out for trouble."

"You definitely do." His mom swatted him with a hand towel. "Now get going. Don't keep the sheriff's department waiting."

He hustled outside. The lingering cold hadn't been dulled by the morning sunshine. His body had grown accustomed to warm and sunny days almost all year round. His Montana upbringing hadn't been erased by Southern California, proven by the heavy coat he'd remembered to put on before heading out.

The drive into town was uneventful. His parents had purchased forty acres of land outside Snowberry and built their dream house upon it. Why had Pops pushed him so hard to find success outside of Snowberry when he had found his own slice of heaven here?

Nicolas parked his vehicle on the street just like he had yesterday. His tension eased at the sight of Kayla. He exited and strode over to where she stood. "How are you holding up?"

She shrugged. "I woke up this morning hoping this had all been a nightmare. Apparently, it's all real."

"Let's go inside before you freeze. Why were you waiting outside?" He held open the door for her to enter.

"I didn't want to be in there by myself."

She wouldn't be alone as long as he was there. He might not be around for much longer, but he'd make the most of their time together. "I imagine after what happened the last time, you're expecting someone to jump out at you."

The sound of a car pulling into the driveway caught his attention. Christina had arrived. He had so many things to say and not enough minutes left alone with her. "How's Olive?"

"She woke up a few times last night with nightmares. My mom is watching her. They're going on a walk to search for the Easter bunny. I made sure a sheriff's deputy would be close to keep an eye on them. I'll pick up some of her things while I'm here. Having familiar toys and clothes may help her feel more comfortable."

"Olive is lucky to have you as her big sister." He'd

grown up with three sisters and only appreciated their presence in his life after reaching adulthood.

"We will learn together." Kayla picked at a loose string on the collar of her coat. "My life in Colorado Springs is not set up for me to care full time for a pre-schooler. I'll have to stay in Snowberry for at least a few weeks to figure everything out." Distress was etched on her face.

He rubbed her arms, wishing he could do more. Be more to her than an ex-boyfriend who'd broken her heart. "The important thing is she's cared for by people who love her."

The door to the kitchen opened, and Detective Reimer walked in. She wore jeans and a heavy sheriff's department jacket. Before moving into the kitchen, she wiped off her boots on the rug by the door. "Good morning. Thanks for meeting me here, both of you. I apologize for not being able to come yesterday. The crime scene at the motel took longer to process than I expected. Partially due to a delay in the tech team from Missoula."

Kayla's face paled. "Do you have any idea who killed Trevor?"

"Not yet," Detective Reimer said. "A few of the motel guests gave a description of a black truck leaving the motel shortly after the gunshots were heard. A black truck was found abandoned on a road near Snowberry. The truck was stolen early yesterday morning. It could have been used by our shooter. It's been secured at the sheriff's department for processing."

"A black truck ran me off the road yesterday on my

way to the motel." Kayla wrapped her arms around her body.

"Let's review the details of that incident in greater depth when I take your statement," Detective Reimer said.

"Any idea on motive?" Nicolas's gaze followed Detective Reimer—or Christina, as he'd known her in high school—as she moved around the kitchen, taking in the mess.

"There was a break-in and robbery two nights ago at the Snowberry Historical Museum." Detective Reimer spun around to face them. "The necklace and diamonds mentioned yesterday were part of the inventory stolen."

Kayla's eyebrows rose. "Do you believe Trevor robbed the museum? Was he killed for the jewels?"

Nicolas struggled to fit together the man who'd been working to turn his life around with someone who'd pull a heist. Why would Trevor throw away all his progress? He'd wanted to be a part of making his community better. Had he slipped? The prospect sickened Nicolas.

"Trevor worked at the museum as a maintenance technician. He knew the layout and security system." The detective motioned for Kayla and Nicolas to follow her into the living room. "As you can imagine, our county sheriff's department normally doesn't see this much action. Lately, though, we've had an uptick in crime. There have been sightings of higher level criminals in the area. My focus is on solving what happened here yesterday, the robbery and murder, whether they are all connected or not. And whether they're connected to any other recent events or not."

Kayla rubbed her forehead. "Trevor stuck with petty crimes and being the town drunk. Maybe he needed more money and robbed the museum."

"Don't convict your dad just yet. We need evidence, and we have nothing solid tying Trevor to the robbery." Detective Reimer pointed to the sofa, then pulled a kitchen chair into the living room. "I'd like to take a statement from each of you regarding yesterday's events. Then I'll take a look around the house. The crime scene techs won't be able to make it over here until tomorrow. We're running up against the weekend and Easter, but it's important to look for fingerprints or any evidence that Trevor was involved in the robbery."

Positioned on the sofa beside Kayla, he listened as she gave her statement. While she spoke, he found his gaze returned to her folded hands resting on her lap. Once upon a time, he'd held her hand, and it had fit perfectly with his. As they strolled down the sidewalk of downtown Snowberry on their way to the movie theater with fingers entwined, he'd been happy. One of the few times in his life he'd felt content.

When his turn came, Nicolas reported the facts of yesterday—why he'd come to Trevor's house, his unsuccessful chase of Kayla's attacker, the near fatal accident he'd witnessed while trailing Kayla on the way to the motel, the scene once they arrived at the motel and finding Trevor's body inside the room.

Detective Reimer snapped closed her notebook and stood, stretching her legs. "I'm going to walk through the house and look around."

"I'd like to take some of Olive's belongings," Kayla

said. "Have you been able to contact Paula, Olive's mom?"

"No. Since she's no longer a legal parent, we won't attempt tracking her down. If you'd like to inform her of Trevor's passing, you can. Social services will be in contact with you soon." Detective Reimer headed in the direction of the bedrooms. "Once I'm done looking in Olive's room, you can get whatever you need in there."

Sensing the tension radiating off Kayla, Nicolas wrapped an arm around her shoulders. "They have no evidence Trevor was involved with the robbery."

"But it's obvious he was involved." She gritted her teeth. "How could he be so stupid? He was supposed to be caring for his daughter, not committing a felony." Kayla pushed up to her feet, sending Nicolas's arm sliding off her and down onto the sofa. "I used to be the daughter he was supposed to be caring for, but instead, he'd leave me with the neighbor lady so he could go drink and get high with his buddies. You said he'd changed and so did my mom, but people like Trevor don't change."

His own past was full of mistakes. Too many to count. Time and again, God had offered forgiveness and a hand up. If he couldn't believe Trevor was worthy of a second chance, then he couldn't believe it for himself either. Now was not the time to argue the issue with Kayla. "Let me take you for coffee after we're finished here. I'd like a chance to catch up with you." A few months ago, he'd gotten Kayla's phone number from Trevor, and he had meant to contact her. Blame his insecurity, but he'd never made the call. How does a person start that conversation after their history and the amount of time that had passed?

"I don't think that's a good idea." She spun toward the sound of footsteps.

Detective Reimer appeared. "You're all clear to go into Olive's room. Just try not to touch anything you don't have to." She returned to her search of the other rooms.

"Kayla, you're shouldering a heavy burden. I want to help." He should go back to his parents' home, spend Easter with his family and then head back to Los Angeles. He had business to attend to and a full schedule for the coming weeks. Kayla had been a friend. She'd patiently sat with him while he struggled with math problems and other homework. Her tutoring had been the reason he'd was eligible to play football his junior and senior year. During his time in the army, he'd discovered he was dyslexic, then learned to work with his brain instead of fighting it. Nicolas might have blamed Kayla for what happened the night of his injury, but years later, he acknowledged she was blameless. Without her, he might not have finished high school.

She sighed. "I'm grateful you were here yesterday. But there's nothing more you can do. This is a job for law enforcement."

"I can help watch your back, make sure Olive is kept safe. I don't mean to frighten you, but whoever killed Trevor is still out there. If they think you know where the stolen necklace and diamonds are, they may come after you." The thought of Kayla caught in the crossfire reinforced his determination.

"I have no idea where they are." She glanced around the room as if searching for a flash of diamonds to give away the hiding spot. "Trevor said in his voicemail message yesterday that he had something he wanted me to take to nonlocal law enforcement. If he was referring to stolen jewels, he never had the chance to hand them over."

A flash of movement outside caught his eye, and Nicolas went to the picture window to get a better look. A teenager rode a bike down the street. He stopped in front of Trevor's mailbox. He appeared innocent enough, except that Nicolas wasn't accepting anything at face value right now. The teenager pulled a box from out of his backpack and slipped it inside the mailbox.

"I'm going outside to see what that kid just put in the mailbox." He sped to the front door. "Stay here."

"Why not tell Detective Reimer and let her check?" Kayla gripped his arm and pulled until he faced her.

He momentarily became lost in her large blue eyes. How had he messed up so badly that he hadn't enjoyed the sight of Kayla every day since high school? He'd keep her safe now. His urgency to get out to the mailbox returned. The teenager was still there, zipping up his backpack. Nicolas had to get to the kid before he rode away. "I'll be right back."

Kayla loosened her hold, and he slipped out the door.

"Hey," he yelled. "What are you doing? What did you put in there?"

Startled, the teenager reset his hold on the handlebars and pedaled away.

Nicolas's stride increased to a jog. People didn't flee

unless they had something to hide. He reached the end of the walkway. The moment his foot hit the sidewalk, a loud roar pierced his ears. Fire flashed toward him. Then his world blackened.

Kayla raced outside after Nicolas but couldn't react quickly enough. The blast caught her off guard, knocking her off the front stoop. She tumbled down the stairs and landed on a patch of brown grass. Her ears rang, and she pressed her hands over them to muffle the sound. She blinked, trying to soothe the sting of tears.

Nicolas! her mind screamed. He'd been close, too close. If he was hurt—or worse… Kayla halted her anxiety-producing theories. She pushed herself back onto her feet. Her vision narrowed in on Nicolas's large form sprawled on the front lawn. He'd always seemed indestructible to her. *Please let him be okay.*

The front door swung out, and Detective Reimer sprinted out, barking orders into her cell phone. She skidded to a stop by Kayla. "Are you hurt?"

Kayla shook her head. "No. Nicolas was near the blast."

"Emergency services are on their way. Stay here." Detective Reimer left Kayla with firm instructions before heading to Nicolas.

Nicolas would be all right. He had to be. The alternative clawed inside her. When she saw him move, rolling onto his back, she exhaled a long sigh. Her knees gave out and she lowered onto a concrete step. Every muscle in her body trembled.

Flames engulfed the area around where the mailbox once stood. Sirens wailed. Help was on its way.

Detective Reimer had stopped to check on Nicolas before giving chase in the direction Nicolas had pointed—where the kid on the bike had rode away. Kayla staggered across the lawn. She dropped onto her knees and stared at his face. It was smeared with dirt and soot, and a small laceration bled by his temple. Still handsome, though, and still very much alive.

"You should move farther away from the fire." Kayla brushed a piece of dirt off his forehead. "Are you able to move?"

"It is getting a little warm." His grin created a twinkle in his eyes. He propped himself up on his elbows and grimaced. "Can you help me?"

She hooked her arms under his shoulders and pulled, grunting with the effort. "You're heavy."

"Built like my grandfather, who was a champion Greek wrestler." Using momentum, he pushed back on his heels and moved with Kayla until they were a safe distance from the blast area.

She caught sight of the colorful thread bracelet around his wrist. "You still have it." Raw emotion squeezed her chest. Nicolas had held on to her gift. He hadn't forgotten their youthful connection. She lifted her right arm and presented her matching one.

"Of course. This piece of fine jewelry is one of my most valued possessions." He grinned. "Handmade and one of a kind." Nicolas glanced at Kayla's wrist. "Correction, two of a kind."

She'd found her bracelet inside the jewelry box in

her old bedroom and tied it on her wrist last night. The memory of weaving the threads together to produce something strong and beautiful had provided a moment of serenity. Did his bracelet remind Nicolas of happy times as well?

The Snowberry Fire Department pulled up, and several firefighters hopped out of the engine. They went to work putting out the flames. Several other sheriff's deputies had arrived. Detective Reimer returned, looking flushed and out of breath.

Nicolas reached over and handed Kayla a crumpled envelope with her name scribbled on the front. "I saw this on the grass right after the explosion."

With her heart pounding, she tore open the envelope and removed the single sheet of paper. Only a handful of words were written on its surface: *Hand over what's mine or you're next.*

SIX

Kayla's fingers burned while pinching the corner of the paper. Her vision blurred. Another threat. Murdering Trevor hadn't produced the stolen treasure. She would hand over the loot in a heartbeat if she knew where it was. Especially with Olive in danger.

Nicolas removed the note from her frozen grip, folded it and returned it to the envelope. "We'll hand this over to the sheriff's department."

"I can deal with the threat to me, but what about Olive?" she choked out. "I need to call my mom." Kayla fumbled in her jacket pocket, which she found empty. Had she left her phone inside? She scanned the ground where she'd been at the time of the explosion. No sign of her cell phone. Her mom had to be warned.

The flames had been mostly extinguished. A few stragglers ate up patches of dry grass. A medic approached Nicolas with a bag in hand. He began the examination by asking a series of questions. Judging from the clarity of Nicolas's answers, he'd be all right. Shaken up and sore, surely. The bomb planted in the mailbox could have killed him. If he'd been closer, it might have. A sharp reminder that danger followed an association with her.

More sirens pierced the air, announcing the arrival of the sheriff's vehicle. Sheriff Gomez climbed out of the driver's seat and set a tan Stetson on his dark haired head. He stood still for almost a minute, assessing the scene. Detective Reimer approached and appeared to provide an accounting of events. He listened, then gave her a sharp nod. His attention turned to Kayla, and the sheriff strode over to where she stood.

The hard look in the sheriff's eyes turned her stomach. She'd seen that look before from him. Sheriff Gomez was not a fan of Trevor Swartz, which had led him to be suspicious of Kayla when she was a high school student. Not like she'd ever done anything to earn his scrutiny. On the contrary. She had been a model student and citizen. Facts sometimes didn't matter though.

Seeing Nicolas was in good hands, she took a few steps to meet Sheriff Gomez. Her knees were still wobbly, but the ground had stopped spinning.

"Kayla Swartz." Sheriff Gomez held out a hand. His thick fingers encircled her hand and pressed. "I haven't seen you around these parts in years. What brings you back to Snowberry?"

She swallowed the lump in her throat. "My father asked me to come." Why was she sweating? She'd done nothing wrong. Her spine straightened. "But he was murdered, and someone planted a bomb in his mailbox. What's going on?"

The sheriff's bushy eyebrows shot up. "I was hoping you could tell me. You showed up at the motel right after the murder and happened to be nearby when the bomb went off."

"I arrived in town yesterday to get my sister, Olive." She crossed her arms. "She was at the motel when Trevor was shot. She's my concern."

"Trevor is our primary suspect in the museum robbery." Sheriff Gomez glanced at the house behind her. "Everything stolen is still missing. That's approximately a million dollars in gemstones and gold, which had been donated by the town's founding family more than a hundred years ago."

The sheriff's biases might have been the reason Trevor did not want to involve him. "Are you certain Trevor is the thief?" He'd stolen low-end goods for drug money and gambled to pay off debts. Then again, she hadn't spent much time in Snowberry or around Trevor to have a good understanding of what he'd been up to lately. Judging from the accounts from her mom and Nicolas, Trevor had cleaned up and gone straight. Something Kayla had a hard time believing.

"Initial indications show Trevor was likely the culprit," Sheriff Gomez replied with a confident air. "If you know where the stolen goods are, you need to tell me immediately. Finding the museum's stolen property is our top priority."

"Not finding out who murdered a resident of your town?" She ground her teeth so hard they threatened to crack. "I have no idea where the necklace and diamonds are."

"How do you know what was stolen?" He drummed his fingers on his thigh in a rapid beat.

"Detective Reimer." She inched closer, almost standing toe to toe with the lawman.

Nicolas appeared at her side, wearing a bandage on his temple and a frown on his mouth. "Are you really investigating or simply pinning the crime on a dead man?"

Her jaw hung slack. Backup had arrived.

Sheriff Gomez had been top lawman around the county for almost thirty years. People didn't challenge him. Until today.

"Excuse me?" The sheriff pinned his dark gaze on Nicolas. "And you are?"

"Nicolas Galanis." He offered a handshake. "Gray Wolf Protection Services, based out of Los Angeles. I'm home visiting my family for Easter. Kayla is a longtime friend." His enjoyment of watching the sheriff's face flash with recognition temporarily eased the throbbing pain in his head.

"Nicolas Galanis. You were the star quarterback for the high school team about fifteen years ago." Sheriff Gomez's gaze flicked to Kayla before reverting to Nicolas. "I'm shocked you'd want to hang around a Swartz again, given how that bar fight involving Trevor ended your season and a promising career. We all pinned you as a future NFL first draft pick."

Nicolas's body flashed with heat, mostly due to anger. How dare the sheriff use what happened more than a decade ago to put a black mark on Kayla. "I'm not here to reminisce. Kayla is a victim. Her father was murdered, and her half sister was there in the room when it happened." He pushed the envelope with the threatening note into the sheriff's hand. "Whoever de-livered the bomb left this too. What's being done to catch the perpetrator?"

Sheriff Gomez took a moment to read what was in-side. He waved over Detective Reimer and passed it to her. "Give this to the crime lab team and see if they can pull prints. Did you get an ID on the person seen riding a bike?"

"I think it was one of the Harrison kids," Detective Reimer said. "There's a deputy headed to their house now. The patrols at your mom's house will be more frequent. I'll see about round-the-clock surveillance."

"Not sure if we have the resources for a twenty-four-hour detail, but we'll keep an eye on the house and you. Meanwhile, Kayla, stay available. Call with any new information." With a nod, Sheriff Gomez tipped his hat, then sauntered back to his department vehicle.

"The Harrisons are a good family," Kayla inter-jected. "Or at least they were when I lived in Snowberry. How did one of their kids get involved with planting explosives?"

"That's what I mean to find out." Detective Reimer studied Nicolas's face. "Go to the medical clinic to be checked over. Today," she said, adding to the order. "I'll be in touch with any news, Kayla."

"Thanks." Kayla's shoulders slackened. "This has all been a bit…much."

"It has, even for me." Detective Reimer slipped the envelope inside an evidence bag. "There's a specialist that conducts forensic interviews with children. She's located in Helena and can't get here for a few more days to talk to Olive. Until then, don't ask Olive leading questions or offer insights on what she may have witnessed. If she does offer information on her own, jot it down, and please let me know at once. I agree with Sheriff Gomez that you should lay low until we wrangle in everyone involved." She gave Kayla a pat on the back before heading back to what was left of the mailbox and post.

Kayla rubbed her hands down her face, then scrubbed her eyes with her fists. She peered up at Nicolas through weary eyes. "You shouldn't have defended Trevor. Sheriff Gomez is going to unfairly lump you in with me and Trevor. He may even write you a ticket for disorderly conduct again."

"I don't care what he thinks." Noticing her stance appeared slightly unsteady, he took her arm and guided her back into the house. "The sheriff had no right to demean you. And he has no proof Trevor was involved in the robbery."

"You were the town golden boy. Don't drag yourself through the mud on my account." She headed to Olive's bedroom.

He followed, furious at her stubbornness. With every attempt to help, she put up new roadblocks. "Kayla." He took hold of her shoulders and spun her to face him. "Do you think I care what anyone in this town besides my family thinks about me?"

"I'm sure your family thinks you shouldn't be with me too." She sniffled, and dampness glistened in her eyes. "You could have been killed outside. Being with me puts you in danger."

Despite her sharp tone, her concern about his welfare warmed his chest. At least she cared. Cared enough to push him away in an attempt to keep him from being hurt. "Let me help you with Olive's things, and then I can come over to your mom's house. I can stay as long as you like."

She shook her head, and her ponytail swung back and forth. "You're getting involved with a danger that you can walk away from."

"I couldn't walk away from what you're going through."

One corner of his mouth lifted at the determined tilt of her chin. "My job is to protect people. Someone wants to harm you and Olive. Don't ask me to go back to my parent's place and dye Easter eggs while your family is in danger."

Kayla shrugged out of his hold. She hustled to the bed and tossed articles of tiny clothing in the duffle bag with *Olive* stitched on the front. "What did Trevor do that made you believe he'd changed? I don't understand how you could have forgiven him. You lost everything because you stepped into that fight."

"I didn't lose everything." The only thing lost that still stung was Kayla, but that was his own fault. "Trevor sent me a letter about a year ago. Part of his recovery program included making amends to people he'd harmed in the past. I guess he thought I fell into that category due to my broken arm earned defending him." Nicolas lowered onto the foot of the bed. Olive's room was filled with toys a little girl would love. Her bed was covered with a fluffy pink blanket. Stuffed animals concealed most of an upholstered chair in the corner. Trevor had made a lot of effort to create a welcoming space for his daughter. "He asked if we could meet sometime when I was in Snowberry. We got together once at a coffee shop. It didn't take me long to accept that he was a different person than the one I knew of back in high school."

"He never apologized to me." Kayla pointed a finger at her heart. "If Trevor really wanted to make amends, he should have started with me."

He read the pain etched on her face and wished to wipe it away. "You're right. Maybe he was afraid if he tried and failed, he'd sink back to a place he had just crawled out of. I didn't know him well, but I trusted his intentions."

"His intentions?" Kayla zipped up the duffle bag and tossed it over her shoulder. "Do you know how many times I trusted his intentions and was repaid with disillusionment? Too many to count. I had to harden my heart to him, or I'd have no heart left. And now, I hear all these stories about Trevor turning over a new leaf. But the sheriff still thinks Trevor is guilty because of his past. If he worked at the museum, then he must be guilty. All I know is Trevor was murdered and someone will kill again if they don't get what they think Trevor stole."

"Which is why I want to come back with you and stay." Standing, Nicolas pleaded his case. "I can't solve the crime because I'm not a cop, but I can keep you and Olive safe."

Her head snapped in his direction. "You want to help? Then help me figure out who is behind the shooting and the bombing, and if they're related to the missing jewels. You heard Sheriff Gomez. The department's priority is recovering the millions of dollars of stolen goods."

"Do you think Trevor might be innocent?" Nicolas's faith in Trevor had been withering, mostly due to circumstantial evidence. What had started as a favor to a man he thought deserved a second chance had grown into a fierce desire to protect his daughter. Old feelings for Kayla stirred, and Nicolas began questioning if keeping close to her was a good idea for his heart. As soon as the threat ended, he'd return to his business. He had obligations at home, and they didn't leave time for romance, especially a long distance one.

Positioned in the open doorway of the bedroom, Kayla fiddled with her car keys. "It doesn't matter if I believe he's innocent or guilty. I plan on finding out the truth. Are you coming or not?"

His heart skipped. Blame the sensation on his thirst for solving a mystery. Not on the heated way Kayla looked at him right now. A look that sent a jolt of energy through his veins from his head to his toes. Nicolas trailed behind her, knowing not doing so was no longer an option.

Have I completely lost my mind? Kayla asked herself the question for the hundredth time. What had possessed her to try to solve a burglary and murder? Mainly, she didn't trust the sheriff's department and its leader's narrow focus. Taking action herself might be the only way to remove the threat hanging over their heads.

Not only did she think she could get a jump on the possible culprits threatening her and Olive, but she'd asked Nicolas to join her. Bless him, Nicolas wanted to help, but being around him did strange things to her brain. Kayla didn't need any more reminders of how hopelessly in love she'd been with Nicolas during high school. Even after fifteen years of healing, the ghostly sensation of her broken heart lingered. Given Nicolas's background and profession, she'd be a fool not to accept his offer. Or maybe she was foolish in thinking she could keep a professional demeanor with him and not grow attached again.

She planned to meet Nicolas at the museum in an hour. He headed over to the town's medical clinic while she'd rushed to her mom's house to check in.

"Don't open the door for anyone," Kayla instructed her mom. "Call me if you notice anyone suspicious loitering outside. Don't hesitate to call 911."

"You're scaring me." Her mom pressed a hand over her heart. "If you're worried about someone hurting Olive, then you're in danger too. Don't put yourself in harm's way any more than you already have."

"Nicolas will be with me, as long as he's given a clean bill of health by the doctor." His injuries from the bomb blast could have been so much worse. *Thank you, God, for protecting him.*

The sound of Nicolas's name brightened her mom's

face. "You two have been inseparable these last couple of days."

She shook her head. "Only due to necessity." Kayla didn't wish to plant seeds of romance into her mom's fertile imagination. "He wants to clear Trevor's name and keep watch over the situation. That's all."

"That's all, huh?" her mom carried a plate holding a peanut butter and jelly sandwich into the living room. "Olive and I are working toward eating at the table. Right now, I'm happy she's eating at all." Her mom set down the plate on the coffee table and motioned Olive over.

The ever present purple bunny was tucked underneath Olive's arm. She sat on her knees and munched on the bread while keeping her gaze fixed to the cartoon on the TV.

Sasha rested on the floor, not exactly begging but using her big brown eyes to transform cuteness into treats.

"How's she been this morning?" Kayla asked in a whisper.

The adults moved away from Olive to the other side of the room. "She seems happy. For most of the morning, she played with your collection of dolls. I found them in a box stuffed at the back of your closet." Kayla's mom wiped her hands on the dish towel slung over her shoulder. "Olive will not be parted from Hoppy, her stuffed bunny. Trevor gave it to her the moment she arrived at his house for good."

"Did Trevor mention where Olive's mom may have gone?" Maintaining Olive's sense of security was top priority. There'd been a good reason Paula had her daughter removed from her care, then signed away her parental rights. Trevor hadn't gone into specifics with Kayla, but she knew enough to keep Paula away from Olive, at least for the immediate future. Perhaps someday when their lives settled, Kayla would find a way to contact Paula.

"Trevor had no idea. Paula had a new boyfriend, who she'd brought with her for a recent visit. The two were staying in a motel in Snowberry, then took off again." Her mom fingered a lock of hair that had escaped Kayla's ponytail and tucked it behind Kayla's ear. "You are Olive's blood. I understand a bond through Trevor isn't a dream come true, but no one will love and care for her like you will."

She gazed at Olive as a strong tug pulled her heart. Of course she loved her. Kayla had loved her half sister from the moment they'd first met last autumn. But to become a full-time caregiver scared her half to death.

"I know what you're thinking. Solve one problem at a time," her mom said. "Olive is safe here with me. I just saw a sheriff's vehicle drive by. I'd watch Olive from time to time when Trevor needed a sitter. It's nice to have a little one around again."

"Thanks for everything." Kayla kissed her mom's cheek. "I need to meet Nicolas at the museum soon. How long did Trevor work there?"

"Oh, about three months. He was proud of that job." Her mom smiled with affection. "He took me on a tour of the museum once, even though I've been there a dozen times."

"It still amazes me that you never shut him out of your life." If being Trevor's child was hard, how difficult had it been for his wife turned ex-wife? Kayla had never heard her mom speak ill of Trevor, despite being completely justified in doing so. Her mom had come to his aid many times, even after their divorce.

"No one is perfect, honey. Not me or you or your dad. God looks past my imperfections and loves me anyway. I want to be a reflection of His love."

"You are." Kayla glanced once more at Olive, still watching TV with Hoppy propped at her side. "I'll call you with any updates."

"Be careful out there," her mom called out as Kayla walked to the door. "And don't forget your coat. I heard a spring storm is approaching."

More than one storm hung over Snowberry as Kayla left the house. She prayed for shelter from the impending destruction. She prayed for Olive, her mom and Nicolas. She prayed for a forgiving heart.

Kayla drove to the museum, keeping a running conversation with God. Could she find it in herself to forgive Trevor, even if he was responsible for putting these recent events into motion?

SEVEN

Nicolas turned onto Washington Street. The downtown section of Snowberry stretched out before him. If he kept going in this direction, the street would lead to wide plains that curved around the north edge of town. Farther in the distance, a snowcapped mountain range pushed up to the sky. Gray clouds were moving in from the west, a sight matching his mood.

The buildings that made up downtown Snowberry hadn't changed much since he moved away. Growing up, he considered Snowberry and, by greater extension, Montana a bubble he'd had to burst and escape from. Serving in the army verified his beliefs. He'd seen a lot of the world and experienced many cultures. He'd admit, Pops had been correct to push him to explore life outside Snowberry. Some part of his small-town upbringing remained, filling a small section of his heart with an urge to settle here. He enjoyed life in Southern California, but it didn't feel like home. This rugged land called to his soul. Someday, he might move back, build a log cabin on several acres and spend his days fly-fishing. Someday—when he was ready to retire.

After parking in the lot for the historical museum, he waited for Kayla to arrive. He remembered coming here on school trips. The antique jewelry display hadn't kept his attention as much as the weapon and gun displays. As a boy, he'd pictured carrying one of those old-time pistols in a holster around his waist, waiting on some dusty street for the bad guys to ride into town.

Kayla pulled into the spot beside him, then exited her car. The breeze tossed her hair, and she brushed strands off her face to uncover her eyes.

"How's everything at home?" he asked.

"Olive is being spoiled, and my mom is loving every minute of it." She grinned. "I told my mom to stay inside and call 911 if she notices anything suspicious. Let's hope she doesn't need to."

"They'll be fine. Trevor's house appears to be the main target." He held open the door, then entered the museum lobby behind Kayla.

"How was the checkup at the doctor?" She gazed up at him with concern in her eyes.

Rolling his neck, he appreciated the ache of sore muscles. Pain meant he was still alive. "Everything is where is should be. No concussion. I should feel as good as new in a few days." He looked around the museum's entryway. The decor hadn't changed since the last time he'd come here. "What's your plan?"

"Ask questions. Figure out how Trevor was perceived here. Learn how complicated it would have been to pull off stealing pieces from this place." She walked up to the information desk.

A middle-aged woman sat on an office chair working

on a crossword puzzle. "How may I help you?" Her gaze wandered from Kayla to Nicolas, and it stuck there.

"I'm Trevor Swartz's daughter. I heard he worked here."

The woman, whose name tag read Francine, gasped. "Oh, you poor thing. I'm so sorry. You must be simply devastated."

"Yes." Kayla glanced at the ground. "I live in Colorado and hadn't seen him much lately. I was hoping to talk to some of his coworkers to get a better understanding of how he was doing recently."

Nicolas kept silent, admiring Kayla's angle at collecting information.

Francine stood and rounded the desk, taking Kayla's hand. "He really cared about his job. Not many people do these days." She cleared her throat. "I know what people are saying, that he robbed the museum, but I don't believe it. Only last week, Trevor brought his little girl, your sister, to the museum. He looked so proud."

"Did he mention having money problems?" Kayla inquired.

"Not to me. Like I said, I firmly believe he's innocent. Once they catch the real culprit, your dad's name will be cleared." Francine nodded her head as if she were an explanation mark.

"Thank you. Can I have two tickets, please?"

"You both go right on in. Most of the museum is closed off. It's like the *CSI* show in there."

"I imagine." Nicolas took note of the crime scene tape inside the museum.

He and Kayla entered the large open space that held the first exhibit—*Montana During the Ice Age*.

"The cavemen diorama always fascinated me." He pointed to figures clothed in animal fur, roasting fake meat over a fake fire.

"They creep me out." Kayla shivered. "It's their eyes. They're following me." With a chuckle, she moved along. "I still can't get over the fact that Trevor held a job for three months and people here actually liked him."

"See, good things can happen." Nicolas's time with Kayla was proof of that. "No one is beyond a second chance."

"Not everyone around here liked Trevor Swartz," a deep voice boomed from somewhere nearby. A man who appeared in his thirties, with thin brown hair on the top of his head, marched toward them. "The man single-handedly ruined my museum."

A woman kept pace at his side. She had a medium build and was dressed in a pencil skirt, white blouse and heels. Her red hair was twisted into a French knot at the base of her neck.

"Excuse me." Nicolas positioned his body between Kayla and this new arrival. He didn't like the intense energy this man was giving off. "You're speaking to Trevor's daughter."

"My condolences." The flat tone and lack of a handshake or expression of empathy showed the man's true feelings. "Calvin Keith, museum director. The museum is closed for the foreseeable future. Too many people traipsing about, dusting for fingerprints and such. Then we have the lookie-loos. I don't get why we are wasting time and resources and shutting down the museum when we all know who is guilty."

"Do we?" A hostile scowl appeared on Nicolas's face. He made no effort to hide his displeasure. "And you have evidence to back up your charge? Surveillance footage? A witness?"

"The thief turned off the security system and video cameras." Calvin scoffed. "When you're trying to solve a mystery, the most obvious answer is usually correct."

"Sounds like you have the case wrapped up." Kayla arched an eyebrow in apparent sarcasm. "How was Trevor as an employee, overall?"

"Trevor Swartz would have been terminated the Monday after Easter," the woman interjected. "I'm Michelle, Mr. Keith's assistant and head of HR. Letting people go is the worst part of my job but sometimes becomes necessary."

Nicolas wrapped an arm around Kayla's shoulders, wishing to protect her from every arrow the world aimed at her. "What would have been the grounds for his termination?"

"He was late for his shifts more than he was on time," Calvin said, chiming in. "Michelle has a folder filled with violations. No surprise given his past."

Believing the worst of someone was easier when they had a prior record. "Why did you hire him then, knowing his criminal history?"

"I wanted to give him a second chance," Michelle said. "He seemed eager to work here. Now I understand why."

Kayla tensed under Nicolas's touch. "Thanks for your time. We'll see ourselves out," Nicolas said.

"Just a moment." Michelle stepped forward. Her shoes clicked on the polished marble floor. "If you know anything about what happened to the items stolen from our exhibit, let us know. Not only are they extremely valuable, but they were donated by Snowberry's founding family. The insurance inspector believes they can be found, which I deeply desire to be true. The jewelry and gemstones are a part of the town's history. I doubt the value the insurance company reimburses us will be near what they are really worth to us."

"If Trevor did have the museum's property, I don't know what he did with it." Kayla squared her shoulders and turned away.

Nicolas steered Kayla back into the lobby. "Don't let them get to you. It's only natural to be defensive of family."

She spun, facing him. "You know, yesterday I believed Trevor was responsible for this entire mess. He made a living off bad decisions. Of course his last act on this earth was another mistake. But something inside me questions if my resentment has blurred my judgment."

Francine reappeared at her desk and plunked down in her chair. "I see you met Calvin and Michelle. Those two started dating a few months ago. Think they're fooling everyone, but we all know what they do in the dark corners of the museum." She chuckled. "Calvin never gave your dad an honest chance. It's a shame because Trevor really tried his best."

"Thank you." Nicolas approached the desk. "I'm sure Trevor was grateful for your friendship."

Francine wiped tears from her eyes. "It's horrible, what happened to him. If you need anything for his little girl, you just ask." She directed the invitation to Kayla.

"I will," Kayla said with a slight smile. "Take care."

Nicolas exited the museum unsure of what to make of their visit. While some held high opinions of Trevor, others despised him. But was their scorn due to his past or present? "Where to next? Would you like to stop at the bakery? It would be nice to chat and learn what you've been up to since high school."

"Maybe another time." Kayla focused on the street running along the parking lot. Cars and trucks rushed by, spraying water left behind from the rain. "There's another place I'd like to stop before heading back to my mom's. I'll understand if you want to skip this one."

"I'm not skipping anything. You're not getting rid of me until you return home."

Kayla gazed up at him with large blue eyes. "It's Big Sky Tavern. I'm sure some of Trevor's buddies still hang out there. If anyone is going to give me an honest opinion of Trevor's recent activities, it will be his old crew."

A familiar sting shot up Nicolas's spine. Big Sky Tavern had been where the trajectory of his life had changed. He'd gone from hotshot quarterback to a teenage boy standing on the sidelines with a shattered arm and criminal record. His hard feelings were long gone, like dust carried off with a strong wind. Though, the memory of that night still created a visceral reaction.

"Count me in." He held open the car door as Kayla climbed into the driver's seat. Trevor's old friends might be behind his murder, so Nicolas was thankful he'd brought along his handgun. While he wished to avoid using it, he felt better knowing it was within reach just in case. "I'll follow you over there. Promise me that we won't get into a bar fight."

Her lips twitched, perhaps fighting a smile to reflect his wry expression. "You're safe with me, Galanis. Well…that's not entirely true. But I'll try to steer clear of any fights, in a bar or elsewhere."

"It will take more than a bomb in a mailbox to scare me away from you." His heart fluttered. *Be careful. Your feelings for Kayla are more dangerous than a bomb blast.*

As Kayla parked on the street outside of Big Sky Tavern, her cell phone chimed. The number for the sheriff's department flashed on the caller ID. "This is Kayla."

"It's Detective Reimer. I wanted to give you an update on your father's case."

Her heartbeat increased. Nicolas stood on the sidewalk near her car. She gestured to him that she'd join him after the call. "Have you found who murdered him?"

"Not yet." Detective Reimer cleared her throat. "I questioned the kid who placed the package with the bomb in the mailbox. He stated that someone contacted him and offered to pay him two hundred dollars to pick up the box and envelope from a bench in the park, then place it into Trevor Swartz's mailbox. He was instructed to toss the envelope on the ground. I believe he had no idea what was in the package. Whomever called the kid used a burner phone."

"You really think he's not involved?" Her stomach sank. They had to catch a good lead soon. The longer this dragged out, the longer she and Olive were in danger.

"The Harrison boy seemed horrified at what happened. He insisted he had no idea who contacted him."

"So where does that leave the investigation? Or is everyone convinced Trevor is the museum thief and I have the jewels stashed somewhere?"

"Some do, but Trevor didn't murder himself," Detective Reimer said. "His fingerprints were found on the display that housed the stolen items, but he worked there. He could have touched the display case prior to the theft. A neighbor of Trevor's reported that he called around midnight and asked her to take Olive. She had the girl over at her house until the next morning. Unfortunately, that fact does not play in Trevor's favor."

"Oh." She tapped her finger on her chin, contemplating the possible reasons he'd gone out that night. None were good. "Is Olive safe in Snowberry? Should I leave with her until things settle down here?" They could go to Colorado Springs. Bring her mom along. What about Nicolas? He shouldn't be involved in this mess to begin with.

"I'd suggest keeping Olive here so we can continue to keep an eye on both of you. Which brings me to my other update. Olive's mom was seen in Missoula. She and her boyfriend broke into a house and trashed the place. Must have been one heck of a party. When the cops showed up, Paula and her boyfriend ran away on foot. They left the car they'd stolen in the driveway."

"You don't think Paula will come for Olive?" Panic struck at the thought of her sister being pulled back into an unsafe life.

"I don't believe so, but we'll keep an eye out for Paula regardless," Detective Reimer said.

An idea floated in Kayla's mind, and she pulled it closer to examine the possibility. "What if Paula and her boyfriend broke into the museum and stole the necklace and diamonds? They came to town for a visit not that long ago. They might have gone to the museum and seen the sparkling pieces, then decided to steal them, pinning the theft on Trevor."

A moment of silence filled the line. "It's a theory, but there's no evidence. Simply put, nothing and no one is off the suspect list."

Including her? She would never kill another person. That didn't mean she couldn't be implicated. "I'll stay in Snowberry for the time being. I don't want to move Olive again so soon if I don't have to."

"I won't stop until we bring the guilty party to justice," Detective Reimer said with conviction in her voice. "We're still reviewing evidence from the scene. Resources outside our local department have been contacted to assist. Keep safe. We'll talk again soon."

"Thank you." Kayla ended the call, then gripped the steering wheel with both hands. What would it take to halt the madness surrounding her? "Trevor, why didn't you tell me more?" she asked the question to the empty car interior. "Why didn't you help me understand so I could keep Olive safe?" She sniffled back the tears burning her eyes. The neon sign for the bar caught her gaze.

Time to stop crying and toughen up. The crowd inside couldn't view her as weak. She left the safety of her car and approached the front door of the establishment.

"Everything all right?" Nicolas asked when he joined her.

"Detective Reimer called. The teen who delivered the bomb was caught. It doesn't seem like he knew a bomb was inside. A mystery caller offered him cash for his service."

"And like most teenage boys desperate for spending money, he didn't ask questions." Nicolas shook his head. "I hope he's grounded for a very long time."

"Agreed." She reached for the door handle, then halted. "Seems like yesterday we came racing over to this same spot, not knowing what lay in store."

"As I recall, Trevor had just been knocked down." He stared at the concrete at his feet. "All those men were surrounding him. I was afraid they'd kill him."

"I'm sorry you were with me." Years of regret bubbled to the surface. "If I could turn back time and change things, I would."

"I wouldn't. You may have been hurt." Taking her hand, Nicolas lifted it so their joined hands pressed on his chest. "Was I angry? Yes. But I never should have taken my anger out on you, or Trevor for that matter. I'm sorry for hurting you."

Her heart raced. So much had happened between then and now. His apology meant a lot. Knowing he didn't still blame her healed a few of the raw wounds she carried from her youth. "I'm grateful we've repaired our friendship. Let's not dwell on the past. We aren't defined by our history."

"Thank goodness for that." He smiled fully, showing off the small dimples on either side of his mouth.

"Trevor's buddies are not nice people." She couldn't forget some of their faces. Men who'd drunk beers on old sofas in her father's backyard until they passed out. Men who cursed, leered at her whenever she was around and made her dislike her father even more.

God had blessed her throughout her life. Protected her from those bad men and provided a few good ones. Nicolas had been the best, and they'd been brought back together. He was a man who reflected God's love. If only she could learn to reflect that same love to others outside her tight circle of trust.

EIGHT

The smell of stale cigarette smoke and beer hit Kayla's nose the moment she entered Big Sky Tavern. The familiar scents hurtled her back in time. She was, once again, a child shaking her father awake after he'd passed out on the sofa sometime the night before. She blocked out the unsettling memories. Reliving her history with Trevor would not help her figure out the person he was before his death.

Nicolas strolled up to the bar and pulled out a stool. "Make yourself comfortable."

Unlikely. Her stomach soured. She ordered a cola with lemon and disregarded the puzzled look of the bartender, which faded once Nicolas replicated her order.

Their drinks were set before them on the high-gloss bar top. "Don't get many requests for soda without the booze."

She'd only ordered a drink to be polite. Information was what she required. "I'm Trevor Swartz's daughter, Kayla. I'm sure you heard he was murdered yesterday."

The bartender's face fell, genuinely somber. "My condolences. I knew your dad for a long time. We went to high school together. I'm Hank, by the way. Owner of this fine establishment."

Fine wasn't the adjective she'd use. "Did you see Trevor much during the past year?"

"Nah." Frank grabbed a basket of unshelled peanuts and set it on the bar. "Trevor swore he'd cleaned up and gone sober. I didn't believe him at first, but after he left that barstool open for a few months, I started to."

Kayla glanced at the empty seat at the end of the bar. She pictured Trevor slumped over, insisting on one more before stumbling home. "When was the last time he was here?"

"Let's see." Hank scratched his scruffy jaw. "He stopped in two weeks ago, but not for liquid refreshment."

"Then why did he come?" Nicolas inquired. He sipped his drink, looking completely calm but downright lethal if provoked.

"To talk with Manny." The bartender pointed to the table at the back of the room, protected by shadow. "You're the Galanis kid, aren't you? Well, not a kid anymore." His gaze traveled up Nicolas's tall frame. Even seated, Nicolas cut a hard profile. "I remember you playing ball in high school. You ever make a comeback after breaking your arm outside the bar?"

Nicolas scowled. "I joined the military instead. Who is Manny, and why did Trevor want to talk with him?"

"Don't know." Hank shrugged, then picked up a dish rag. Wiping down the already clean bar top, he flicked a glance toward the occupied table. "Getting involved in my patrons' business is bad for my bottom line."

Leaning forward, Nicolas rested his muscular forearms on the bar. "Tell me."

Kayla stared at him, filled with admiration. The man knew how to use his assets.

Beads of sweat covered Hank's forehead. "You gotta understand. Manny, Leon and Trevor go way back. They were a tight crew until Trevor had a change of heart. There was a falling out. That's all I know. When Trevor came in two weeks ago, the guys talked, then started arguing. After a little pushing and getting into one another's faces, Trevor stormed out. I swear, I don't know any more."

"Then I'll ask Manny." Kayla pushed back on the barstool and stood.

"I'd advise against that." Hank stared down at his handiwork with the dishrag. "Trevor's dead, rest his soul, and there's no sense in stirring up trouble."

"I disagree." Nicolas got to his feet as well. "Thanks for your help." He tossed a twenty onto the bar.

Hank swept up the bill and secured it in his clenched hand. "Don't say I didn't warn you."

A shard of ice imbedded into her spine. The back of her neck tingled. *You didn't come this far to back down.* Plus, she had her own personal bodyguard. These barflies would need to be crazy to risk a fight with Nicolas. She hesitated at the thought of him getting hurt again. But Nicolas was charging toward the back table with no reluctance. She hurried to keep up.

Small-town gangsters didn't intimidate him. Nicolas had faced down these types many times. During the fight that night in high school, he'd been bested. The odds had been stacked against him. But bad odds had never stood in his way, which was why he'd suffered a broken arm in high school then a gunshot wound to his femur while he was in the army. By now, he should have learned to mind his business and stay out of battles that weren't his. But as long as Kayla needed him, he'd stay in this fight. Leaving her now would be even more painful than another gunshot.

He approached the table that the bartender had pointed out. Four men reclined on two booth benches facing each other. About a dozen beer bottles littered the table between them. As he came to the table, the four guys peered up at him in unison. "Nicolas Galanis," he said. "I was a friend of Trevor's." Using the past tense hurt.

The one who appeared to be the leader of the pack clenched his jaw and ground his teeth back and forth. Finally, he loosened his lips. "Sorry to hear he's singing with the angels now. Unless he ended up in the other place."

The group at the table chuckled.

Beside him, Kayla tensed, ready to pounce.

"Don't let them get under your skin," he whispered to her. Then he directed his unamused focus at the speaker. "I heard you and Trevor were old pals. I'd think you'd be more upset about his passing."

"We're drowning our sorrows." The man pointed to an empty beer bottle.

He assumed this one was Manny. One of the other guys had a shirt with a name patch stitched to the front.

Leon appeared to be on a lunch break from the auto repair shop. He made a mental note to tell his family members never to take their vehicles to that business.

"He came to speak with you a few weeks ago," he said, pushing on. "What about?"

Manny took a long pull of beer before exhaling. He set down the bottle with a clank. "The bum wanted back in. He'd turned his back, said he wouldn't run with us anymore, and then he came crawling in asking for favors. He needed some extra cash."

"Did you give it to him?" Kayla asked.

Manny looked her over. "You've grown up, kid. Haven't seen you in a long time."

"How observant." Kayla's blue eyes narrowed. "You didn't answer the question."

Nicolas fought against the desire to pick her up and carry her out far away from these men. They didn't deserve to spend a second with Kayla.

"Of course not. I'm not a bank." Manny tapped his fingers on the laminate tabletop. "I sent some work his way. A couple of odd jobs. Nothing to write home about."

"Did he say why he needed the money?" Nicolas caught sight of a bulge underneath Manny's lightweight jacket—likely a gun. At the first sign of aggression, he'd get Kayla out of here. He'd rather flee than get into a shootout.

Silence. Leon coughed. One of the other men opened the top of the beer bottle using the corner of the table.

Manny reclined back in the booth seat. The lump of his gun became more predominant. His hair had, for the most part, disappeared, and a thin band of short mane looped around the back of his head. He dressed like most people in these parts, a casual look that worked for both outdoors and in.

"Look." Kayla pressed the palms of her hands on the table and leaned in. "I just want to know who my father was before he died. I'm sure you know he's accused of stealing from the museum."

"If I would have known he'd planned one last hit, I'd have asked that he cut me in," Leon barked. "Now he's dead and all that bling is missing." Dark eyes fixated on Kayla. "I'll still make a deal. You share the wealth and we'll offer protection."

"She doesn't have the stolen goods." Nicolas gripped Kayla's shoulder and drew her away from the men. "Someone else robbed the museum."

"Right." Manny snorted a laugh. "So why was Trevor shot then? If he had nothing to do with the museum heist, then why was he killed?" Without warning, he jumped up and moved toward Kayla. "Where'd he hide it?"

Nicolas grabbed Manny by his jacket and yanked him away from Kayla. "Back off."

Leon loped out of the booth. Dressed in his stained auto repair shirt and baggy jeans, he appeared less threatening.

Still, Nicolas stayed locked on them all.

"You wanna know who killed your pa?" Leon's question hung in the air.

Kayla looked ready to slap the grin off Leon's face.

"Did you kill him?" Nicolas had no interest in playing games.

"Of course not," Leon said. "We're all law abiding

citizens here. But the law favors those who dance to their music. Trevor danced. He turned into a rat."

"What do you mean?" Kayla's eyebrows pulled together.

"Trevor talked. That's what he means," Manny interjected. "One of the sheriff's deputies was dirty. Trevor testified at his trial. The deputy didn't serve long, only a few months. He got out of jail last week, or so I heard. Could be why Trevor needed the money."

"A payoff to leave him alone?" Nicolas couldn't wrap his mind around the information. Had Trevor been killed by a convicted lawman seeking revenge?

"This deputy lost his job and reputation. You know how a small town can be." Manny pushed back the opening of his jacket, displaying his firearm. "Everybody knows everyone else's business. I'll leave you with this. Your dad had no friends at the end. He turned on us, his crew. No one in town believed he really changed. When he got the job at the museum, I figured at least one person was giving him a second chance. Guess that person is regretting their decision."

Nicolas's heart dropped. Where had he been when Trevor had needed a true friend? He'd been too busy working, building his business. In the end, he answered Trevor's final call, but his help had arrived too late. At least he could guard Kayla and Olive.

"Trevor didn't steal from the museum." Pure rage shot out like lightning bolts from Kayla's eyes.

"Of course his daughter would say that." Manny patted his gun in the holster. "There's a million dollars' worth of gemstones and jewelry missing. Where is it?"

A brief assessment told him that Manny was the only one armed. The two men who remained in the booth seemed uninterested in the conversation. Leon wore no telltale signs of a weapon.

"Put away the gun," Nicolas growled.

Kayla put a hand on Nicolas's chest, using light pressure to urge him not to lunge. She rested her gaze on the men at the table. "We'll leave. If Trevor did have the stolen items, I don't know where they are. If I did, do you think I'd still be in Snowberry?"

Leon snorted. "I'd have flown this coop the second I had my hands on it."

"Watch your back, kid." Manny let his jacket fall to cover the weapon. "You don't want to meet your daddy's fate."

Taking a firm hold of Kayla's arm, Nicolas escorted her away from the men and to the door. Once outside, he looked her over.

Kayla's flushed cheeks matched her trembling body.

"I won't let them hurt you," he soothed, rubbing her upper arms.

"Don't worry about me. Worry about them." She shoved her hands into the pockets of her coat. "I shouldn't have ignored Trevor these past months. He tried to tell me, but I wouldn't listen. I wasn't here when he needed me."

"Yes, you were. You came when he asked for help. You got Olive and are keeping her safe." His chest ached for Kayla. He knew regret all too well.

"Olive. I should get back to her."

He wanted to go with her. She needed space, though.

To be with her family, bond and grieve. He should head home too. "Can I come by tomorrow to check in?"

"Of course." Her body had stopped trembling, and her face relaxed. "It's Good Friday already. I don't have an Easter basket for Olive. And I'm sure she'll want to dye eggs."

"I'm a master Easter egg dyer, as a matter of fact. Call me if you need me, anytime. I'll be over in a flash." Although he had promised his nieces he'd be home to dye some eggs. He hated disappointing people he loved.

"Thanks. I'm praying for a quiet rest of the day. See you tomorrow." She moved toward her car, then turned back to him. "I don't know what I'd do without you."

Should he admit he'd be lost without her too? Best keep his mixed-up feelings to himself. "Protecting others is my job. But you don't need protection as much as backup. I'm grateful to fill the roll."

During the drive home, he considered that years ago, he'd been in love with Kayla. His drive for success had pulled him away. Now commitment to his success nudged him to keep an emotional distance until he returned to California. The love he felt for her was one of a teenage boy, yet still more real than anything he'd felt since.

NINE

Seated on the floor in her mom's living room, Kayla moved her marker—a red plastic gingerbread man—three spots on the game board. After the scene at the bar, she needed calm. Playing a child's game with Olive and her mom proved a good distraction. Instead of picturing guns and angry men, she focused on avoiding landing on a spot on the board that would send her marker plummeting down a slide and back to Start.

"Your turn," she said to Olive.

The little girl picked the top card off the pile. "Red." Her chubby hand gripped her marker and moved it to the correct spot.

"She's smart." Her mom ruffled Olive's hair. "Trevor was teaching her letters."

"Hearing that amazes me." Kayla stretched out her legs. The three of them were assembled around the coffee table. Sasha lay snoring a short distance from Olive.

"Trevor was a complicated man." Her mom took her turn at the game. She landed on a square with a ladder and climbed up three levels. "He had demons from his childhood he carried around for a long time. Becoming the sole caregiver for Olive was a wakeup call."

"How did you not hate him after everything he'd done to us?" She glanced at Olive, who'd become distracted by Sasha's fluffy tail. "He was a horrible husband and father. Your name was dragged through the mud by being associated with him. I left town to get away from the gossip, but you stayed and were a friend to him."

Her mom sighed. "Holding on to bitterness smothers your soul. I'd be lying if I didn't admit I was angry during our marriage and after the divorce. But after some separation, I saw how lost Trevor was. I prayed he'd find his way back to the light. It pained me to see you hurt by his actions, and I'm sorry I didn't do a better job protecting you."

Kayla covered her mom's hand with her own. Love poured out. "You are not to blame."

"Let's be set free of the pain from our past." Her mom watched Olive brush Sasha's tail with her fingers. "The future needs our attention. God has blessed us, Kayla. We've been given this sweet child to care for. Trevor loved both of you so dearly. His heart would be filled with joy knowing Olive is with you."

Trevor had loved her? She'd never felt that sentiment coming from her father. He might have loved booze, drugs and easy money, but not Kayla. Her mind stilled with the spoken opinions of others about Trevor over the last few days. Perhaps removing the vices from his life had left room for love. From all accounts, he'd been a good father to Olive for the time she'd been in his care.

And he had reached out to Kayla recently, but she'd chosen to not respond. Until his plea to help Olive. That request had snuck past her defenses.

"I left a message with school, letting them know I won't be home when classes start after break." Her trip home couldn't be wrapped up in a long weekend like she'd planned. Besides the issue of Olive's guardianship, she had to plan a funeral. "The social worker is coming for a visit at the beginning of next week. I'm meeting with a lawyer about Trevor's will soon. I also should call a funeral home to make arrangements. They can collect Trevor's body once it's been released from the medical examiner."

"I'm here to help." Kayla's mom patted her cheek. "You're not carrying this burden alone."

"I know, and I love you." Seeing Olive had lost interest in the game, Kayla stood up before leg cramps set in. She stretched out her low back, the tightness a reminder she was no longer a teenager.

Olive had moved on from Sasha to the collection of toys in the room. She set Hoppy on a doll-sized chair and began making a meal in the play kitchen.

"I meant Nicolas as well." With a grin, her mom scooted up to the sofa for a more comfortable seat. "He's been devoted."

Kayla's body warmed as she recalled the way he'd gone into full bodyguard mode at the bar. If he hadn't looked so handsome while doing it, she wouldn't have experienced the fluttering in her chest at the memory. Her attachment with him was temporary, which was a good thing. Kayla had learned to be an expert at saying goodbye. Plenty of practice after every time she grew too emotionally close to a man. "Trevor asked for his help before he died. I'm sure Nicolas feels obligated to make sure I stay out of trouble."

Her mom laughed. "Good luck with that. But we both know it's more than obligation. I'm glad to see you not push him away."

"Oh, I've thought about it." She smiled at the recollection of her ineffective efforts. Like trying to coax a starving bull away from a field of tender grass. His personality made it impossible to back down until the job was done. She'd admired that quality while tutoring him in high school and watching him play football. "He's persistent, maybe too much so."

"Just the right amount, in my opinion." Curled up on the sofa, her mom appeared to have grown younger. Could be the glow of nurturing a little one again. "You put up walls to keep people out, especially romantic partners. You didn't have a healthy relationship to learn from growing up. You saw my and your father's failures and believed marriage wasn't a worthy endeavor. I'm so sorry I failed you in that respect."

"My romantic flounderings are not your fault." But her mom was correct in the assessment of Kayla's relationship hang-ups. As soon as things started to get serious, she withdrew. Shortly after, the guy would end their relationship. It was her cycle—one she rode over and over. "I haven't met *the one* yet, that's all." She had, though, in high school. Fate had made sure there was no happy future with Nicolas.

Setting a small plastic plate topped with a fake apple

on the play table, Olive yawned. "Hoppy says she wants to go to bed."

Kayla checked the time. Not officially bedtime yet, but the sleepy look in Olive's eye said she needed rest. "Can you and Hoppy go to your room? I'll come help you get your jammies. Then we'll go to the bathroom to brush your teeth and hair."

Olive took hold of Hoppy's ears and dragged her out of the room. "Don't forget story and prayers," Olive hollered.

"You pick the story to read tonight." Kayla loved cuddling with Olive in bed while reading, just like her mom had done with her when she was a girl.

Her mom spread a blanket over her lap. Outside, thunder rumbled. The rain and wind had been pounding the house for more than an hour. "Trevor read a book and prayed with Olive every night. He even took her to church. We'd go out for breakfast together after the service. Miracles still happen, and I witnessed one every time I saw my ex-husband come through the church doors with his child."

"Most of the people I talked to today believe Trevor is guilty of the museum robbery. They look at me like I know where he hid the valuables." Kayla tensed, remembering the accusations and questions. No one is capable of real change. Wasn't that what she'd said earlier today?

"Most people believed the world was flat a thousand years ago." her mom huffed. "It's true, the evidence points to Trevor."

"If he needed money, he had motive. He worked for

the museum, so he had means, and he asked a neighbor to watch Olive the night of the robbery."

"Opportunity," her mom added. "But he didn't do it. I know this deep in my soul."

Kayla took a moment to dwell on her mom's conviction. "He called, desperate for me to take Olive. He said he had something to turn in to law enforcement. Not our sheriff's department. Why not leave Olive with you if he felt he was in danger? Nothing makes sense." And why had he gone to Manny asking for money and a job? Was Trevor still crooked, or had he been acting as an informant? A rat was how Lenny had described him.

"He called you because you are Olive's blood. I'm the nice lady who sits next to her in church. You're her half sister. You're Trevor's daughter." Sniffling, her mom pulled a tissue out of a nearby box. "Trevor had his faults—don't we all?—but he could be tenacious about things he cared about. Unfortunately for a long time, those things were not healthy. You inherited his tenacity, and he knew that. You're also the smartest person he knew. He didn't trust Olive to anyone but you."

Admittedly, Kayla was hardheaded and stubborn. She'd found those qualities with her father. Any traits shared with Trevor, she'd either dismissed or fought. The last thing she wanted to admit was that she was his daughter in more than name only.

"If he's innocent, I want to clear his name, but not at the expense of Olive's safety." The threat in the envelope on Trevor's front lawn came to mind. "Keep the window shades down and the doors locked." Something they rarely did in Snowberry. A flash of lightning burst through the fabric of the window covering followed by the rumble of thunder. In the distance, a siren sounded. Noises only added to her sense of dread. She peered out the window, and the sight of a sheriff's department squad car parked across the street calmed her heart.

"Ready," Olive called out from the hallway. She'd gone ahead and dressed for bed herself. Her hot pink pajama top was on backward but that was easily fixed. She looked sweet and innocent. Her feet were encased in furry slippers. Hoppy remained secure in her hand.

Would this be Kayla's new nightly routine? Helping Olive prepare for bed, then story time and prayer? Normally, her nights at home were spent in lesson prep, training with Sasha, then lounging on the sofa until bed called. Was she ready to become a full-time caregiver? Did it matter if she wasn't? Ready or not, her life had transformed. Judging from the warm glow in her chest as she helped Olive turn on the faucet to wet her toothbrush, Kayla needed the changes.

The next morning, Nicolas ran a hand over his black hair. He'd woken early, showered, dressed and was standing in the kitchen, assisting his mom with putting away yesterday's dishes.

Pops walked in, adjusting his suspenders at the same moment Mom handed Nicolas a clean casserole dish and pointed to a high cabinet.

"Morning." Pops went straight to his wife and kissed her cheek. "Good to see you're putting this one to work." He hooked a thumb in Nicolas's direction. "I expected him to be gone already by the time I got up."

Nicolas would have been if not for his mom catching him on the way out. He'd stayed to drink a cup of coffee with her before helping with the dishes. His guilt over being away for most of his stay at home had caught up to him. "I told Kayla I'd be over to check on them this morning." He cleared his throat. "Since I didn't get a call from her overnight, I'm assuming all was quiet at their house last evening." Even so, he wouldn't feel settled until he went over there and saw for himself.

His dad took one of the mugs resting in the drying rack. "Are you sure you should be involved in this latest mess with Trevor Swartz?" A rhetorical question— Pops's specialty. "You're always the first to jump in when someone is in trouble, but your mom and I don't want another call from the hospital telling us you've been injured."

"I'm not putting myself in harm's way." At least not on purpose. "You realize a call like that could come at any time, even when I'm in California. Not that it will." He held up his hands in a gesture to calm his mom's expression of distress.

Palms resting on hips, his mom burned him with a stare. "You were almost blown up."

"I'm in more danger playing tag football in the back-yard with the kids than spending time with Kayla." A bit of an exaggeration. The bomb could have maimed or killed him. As of yet, his sisters and nieces only had caused temporary damage.

Humph. She poured another cup of coffee then set the carafe back onto the hot plate. "Don't be cheeky. We're worried."

"Sorry, ma'am." He turned his head in order to hide his slight grin. "Please trust me and my experience."

"Your experience. You mean your years deployed, which gave me these gray hairs?" She gazed at the calendar hanging on the wall. "Do you plan to join us for Easter church service tomorrow and dinner after? Your father wants to dye red eggs, even though it's a few weeks early for Orthodox Easter."

He should promise. It's the reason he'd come home. But Kayla had changed things. If he were being honest with himself, he'd want to be with her even if her world wasn't spinning out of control. "I'll keep you updated about what's going on." That was the best he could do for now.

"I'm holding you to that." She set down her coffee mug, then motioned him forward.

Nicolas obeyed, leaned down and accepted his mother's hug.

She let go, then stepped back. Patting his cheek, she smiled. Her dimples appeared, reminding him of how much he inherited from this woman.

"Can I speak with you before you head out?" Pops motioned toward the door. A request closer to a command.

"Of course." Nicolas put on his outerwear, then followed his dad onto the porch.

Pops continued down the stairs and toward the barn.

Nicolas followed. Once inside the warmth of the barn, he relaxed his guard. He was a grown man who no longer resided at home. He no longer lived in the same state as his parents. Whatever Pops had to say, he could get it out, and Nicolas could turn his concern back to Kayla.

"I don't agree with what you're doing." Pops pulled out a stool from underneath an untidy table and took a seat. "Trevor Swartz and whatever he was up to was no good. Don't go getting mixed up in problems that don't concern you."

Nicolas reclined on a stable wall. "You raised us to help others. When did that change?"

"Not when the other is a criminal." Rubbing his fists on his denim-covered thighs, Pops lifted his chin. "You didn't work hard to own a successful business only to ignore it."

"I'm not ignoring it."

"But you will." Pops snorted. "I know you. You won't be able to leave until the job is completed."

"Kayla is not a job." A job didn't hold his heart like she did. "Why are you so invested in my success? Would you love me any less if I'd turned out to be a complete failure?"

"Of course not." His dad pushed to his feet. "You're my son. My only son. I want what's best for you. I didn't want you to have to settle."

Being with Kayla would not be settling. The exact opposite, actually. "Being happy in one's life doesn't seem like settling."

Pops cheeks flushed red, and he glanced away. "Happiness is important, sure. You were destined for more than a simple life. I knew from the moment I saw you throw a football that you were special."

Nicolas rubbed his forehead. How many more times would he need to listen to this sentiment? "I'm not special. Sure, I had a talent for playing quarterback, but that didn't work out."

"It didn't work out because you were dating Kayla Swartz."

His jaw tightened as he held in his real rebuttal. "Regardless, I've made a good life for myself. My choices have been my own. And I'm choosing to be there for Kayla. She's in danger, and I can't walk away."

"Are you certain?" Pops stepped forward and rested a work-weathered hand on Nicolas's shoulder. They were close to the same height, with Nicolas beating Pops by a few inches. "Your family needs you too."

Nicolas gazed out the barn's door. The morning dew on the grass sparkled in the sunlight. "I'll make it up to you all. Another trip home soon if I have to leave without spending more time together. Trust me. I'm going where I'm needed most."

Pops moved back and released a breath. "I couldn't stop you even if I tried. Go on. You better stay safe, or it won't be me who'll answer to Mom."

"I'll do my best, sir." He chuckled.

"Before you go, how's business?" His dad walked with him outside.

"Business is growing. We just signed clients from Dubai. It's a big contract. One of our largest in terms of scope and fees." A reminder that his trip home had a timeline. In three days, the new clients would arrive in California, and Nicolas would be required to greet them.

Since separating from the military, he and his partner had worked hard to build a solid reputation as Southern California's most elite bodyguard service. Nicolas had invested his savings and years of his life. His future was in California. His past was in Snowberry. And his present seemed stuck in a spider's web of emotional attachments.

"Hope to see you later today." Pops turned toward the house.

"I have a question for you before I go." Nicolas hesitated, searching for the right words. "You and Mom have a good life. You've raised children and are happy together. Why didn't you want that for me?"

His dad scratched at the stubble on his jaw. "You're right. I love your mom and have been happy with my life. But I was young when I got married. It took years for my itch for adventure and for making a name for myself to quiet down. Never went away fully, if I'm honest. In you, I see what could have been."

And there it was—the truth behind every motivational speech and push to succeed. "I'm not you."

"You're happy with your life as it is now?" Pops asked.

Nicolas opened his mouth to say yes. The hollow section in his chest wouldn't let him speak the affirmation. "I'm mostly content, but there's something missing." More like someone.

"Then you better get moving." Motioning Nicolas to shoo, Pops suppressed a grin. "Your missing piece is out there, waiting."

Before getting into his SUV, he texted his partner, wanting to touch base about their newest client.

A situation came up, and I'm not sure I'll be able to leave on Monday.

The group from Dubai will be here Tuesday. Whatever is going on in Montana will have to wait. You have to be back before the clients arrive.

I'll do my best but I can't promise. You might need to handle the initial meetings.

Nicolas cringed when he pushed Send. He pictured his partner, whose personality retained a constant level of stress. This news would send his blood pressure through the roof.

After several minutes, a reply came.

Don't do this to me. Not when we're so close to pushing the business to the next level. You're the partner with charm. You signed this client. Don't disappoint them.

I'll keep you updated.

The communication served as a stark reminder of Nicolas's high-value obligations. His decisions affected the business, and he had more than himself to consider.

On his way to Hillary's house, he stopped at the bakery downtown and picked up coffee and doughnuts. Despite his desire to see Kayla, he took his time. A test of his self-control. When he parked outside the house, he was ready to race to the front door. Only because he was concerned about their safety. Not because he was falling back in love with one of the women inside.

TEN

After devouring one of the doughnuts Nicolas brought, Olive raced around the house in a sugar-induced crazy high.

"This child needs to burn off some energy." Kayla watched her sister hop like a rabbit across the living room. She made a mental note to stock her pantry with healthy snacks. That is, when she finally made it home. "Does Snowberry still have the Spring Festival the day before Easter?"

"Every year it gets bigger. It's at the park this year instead of the rec center because the weather is so nice." Her mom stood in the room, wearing her waitress uniform. "I hate to leave, but my lunch shift at the restaurant starts soon, and another server already called in sick."

"We can handle this." She glanced at Nicolas, who knelt on the floor. Olive had paused her hopping to climb him like a jungle gym. Doubt surfaced. This little girl might get the best of them. "Right?"

"No problem," he mumbled. Olive had stuffed her hand inside his mouth for a hold to crawl onto his shoulders.

Kayla's mom kissed Olive on the cheek before heading out for work.

Kayla locked the door behind her. "Olive could use some fun after the recent trauma. Do you think it's safe to take her to the festival?"

"I don't see why not, as long as we keep a close eye on her and our surroundings." He stood and gripped the girl by the ankles, hanging her upside down. "I'm sure there'll be a law enforcement presence there."

They smiled as Olive's giggles filled the room.

Nicolas gently set her on the carpet. "Who wants to meet the Easter bunny?"

"Me!" Olive squealed, jumping up and down. "Hoppy wants to see the Easter bunny too."

"You feel all right going?" Nicolas asked her.

Judging from the expression of delight on Olive's face, Kayla couldn't say no. "As long as you're with us." She didn't trust the outside world. When they were with Nicolas, the monsters lurking wouldn't seem as scary to Olive.

The weather was sunny and warm for Montana in April. Another cold front was predicted to move in later tonight. Kayla dressed in jeans and a sweater. She brought coats along for herself and Olive in case the temperatures dropped sooner than expected.

Sasha sat by the door, appearing unhappy at being left behind.

They rode in Nicolas's SUV. Olive's car seat was still secured in the back. Flashbacks from two days ago sent her heart racing. She recalled the panic she'd experienced while speeding to the motel and the grief that smothered her on the way home. Her second chance with Trevor had been killed along with him. The only path left to make amends was through Olive. She'd honor her commitment to her sister no matter the innocence or guilt of their father.

The parking lot at the park was full. Nicolas found a spot on a side street. The nice weather had brought out a large crowd.

Kayla's anxiety stirred. A big gathering of people provided cover for someone wishing to do them harm. But there'd also be many witnesses. In truth, they'd be as safe here as anywhere else in town. Keeping Olive locked up at home wasn't an option. Not if Kayla wanted to stay sane. Plus, Olive needed some fun to dampen the distress she'd experienced of the past couple of days. Replace bad memories with good.

She unbuckled the car seat straps, then helped Olive out of the vehicle. Once standing on the ground, Olive took hold of Kayla's hand. Hoppy remained tucked under Olive's arm. The stuffed bunny provided comfort and likely reminded Olive of the man who'd gifted it.

"Where to first?" Nicolas asked as the festival came into view. Nestled in the center of Snowberry, the park held sweeping views of the mountains. Downtown shops and restaurants ran along one side. Scattered ball fields took up most of the area across the way.

Growing up, Kayla had come here often. First with her mom to climb on the playground equipment. Then as a teenager to hang out with friends. She'd met Nicolas here a few times to study, though she had spent more time sketching the cute boy than teaching him algebra and history. She still had her sketches of him in an art notebook. They were a reflection of how she saw him. His handsome face and kind eyes were etched in her mind as permanently as marker on paper. Under one of the tall elm trees by the picnic tables was where Nicolas had asked her out for the first time. She wanted to jump back in time and tell her younger self not to get too hung up on the football star. *Trusting someone with your heart only brings disappointment and pain.*

Her mind back in the present, Kayla glanced around the space filled with people, food stands and activities. "Let's start with face painting. We can work our way around and end up at the Easter bunny. Olive, would you like your picture taken with the Easter bunny?"

Olive stared wide-eyed at the man-sized furry rabbit waving at the nearby children. She whispered something in Hoppy's ear, then nodded. "Hoppy says yes. Bunny won't hurt me."

Kayla's eyes stung as she masked her sadness with a happy smile. "Nicolas and I won't let anyone hurt you either." She made eye contact with Nicolas and saw her emotions reflected in his gaze.

The hard lines of his profile and tall, strong frame advertised Nicolas wouldn't be opposed. He walked close to Kayla and Olive like a bodyguard while they strolled over to the face-painting tent. "What do you want…a butterfly or a flower?"

"That." Olive pointed to a photo of a child's face painted to look like a tiger and roared.

"Are you sure? The butterfly is so pretty." Kayla knelt to put herself at Olive's level.

"Tiger." Olive folded her short arms across her body.

Kayla knew that stance. She'd done it herself on many occasions when digging in her heels. "Okay, tiger it is."

"He gets a butterfly." Olive lifted her head to gaze up at Nicolas.

His eyebrows lifted. "This is for kids, squirt, not for grown-ups."

"Butterfly," came Olive's insistence.

"I think it would look nice on you." Kayla grinned. "Some colorful paint won't diminish your tough-guy image. I promise."

"Fine." He held up his hands. "You win." Directing his gaze down at Olive, he reached for her, then lifted her up. "But you go first."

Kayla remained at a safe distance from the paint brushes and watched as Olive morphed into a fierce tiger and a tiny butterfly emerged on Nicolas's cheek. He must have bribed the artist to make it small.

Once they were finished, Olive leaped out at Kayla, fingers extended like claws.

"You look fierce," Kayla said.

The artist had done a good job coloring around the top of Olive's face like a mask. Her eyes were encircled in orange, white and black.

"And you look like a tough guy with a soft side." If Kayla wasn't careful, his soft side would melt her resolve. "Where to next?"

A natural-born leader, Olive directed Kayla and Nicolas through the game and activity stations. She requested a stop for cotton candy, jelly beans and ice cream.

If Kayla planned to parent Olive, she'd have to learn how to say no.

Finally, after the rest of the festival had been explored, the trio ended at the Easter bunny photo station.

She took Olive and stood in line. This area was busier than the others. Parents and children crowded around to watch the Easter bunny's antics as it posed for pictures with the children.

They reached the front of the line. Kayla paid before escorting Olive to stand next to the Easter bunny.

Olive gave a wide smile to the photographer.

Love and connection flowed. Kayla couldn't imagine a future without her little sister as a part of her everyday life.

While she waited for the picture to print, she instructed Olive to stand next to her. The printer had run out of ink, which needed to be replaced. Her gaze moved around the area while they waited for their picture. Kayla noticed the sideways glances aimed at her, the narrow-eyed looks of judgment and the whispers. She could only guess what was being said. Speculation whirled in the air. The museum theft and Trevor's murder were big news in a town that didn't see much crime. How many people here assumed Kayla knew where the jewels were located?

"Here you go." The photography assistant handed Kayla a colored picture.

"Thanks." Despite all the awful events that had surrounded her, seeing this photo of a smiling Olive was a balm to her soul.

"Are you ready to go?" she asked Olive, who was

no longer waiting at her side. "Olive," she called out. "Olive, where are you?"

No reply.

Panic hit like a lightning bolt. Olive was nowhere in sight.

When Nicolas heard the terror in Kayla's voice while calling Olive's name, his adrenaline spiked. The conversation he'd been having with a former football teammate came to an abrupt end. He found Kayla, turning in a circle and trembling.

"I took my eyes off her for only seconds," she sobbed. "I can't find her."

He scanned the crowd, searching desperately for the girl. "Stay here in case she comes back. I'll walk around and look for her. We'll find her."

Kayla bobbed her head. "I have my phone. Let me know the second you see her. I'll do the same."

Nicolas jogged off. His military training kicked in. He'd specialized in combat search and rescue. He knew how to read a battlefield for injured soldiers and enemy danger. Locating a small child in a busy city park meant the clues looked different.

Olive could have wandered off. Many sights, sounds and smells here could capture a child's attention. Or, the worst-case scenario, Olive had been snatched. *Please don't let that be the case.* She'd been in the same room when her dad was shot, but she'd been hiding in the closet. The shooter might not want to leave any loose strings.

"Olive," his booming voice sounded. "I'm looking

for a three-year-old girl whose face was painted like a tiger. Have you seen her?" His question was directed to anyone within earshot.

No one had. He moved on. When he reached the far end of the park, he spun around and checked his phone. Kayla hadn't called or texted, which meant Olive was still missing.

He studied the parking lot and the cars in the vicinity. He strained to hear the sound of a child in distress. Too many people. Too many sounds.

"Olive," he shouted again. Desperation turned his blood to ice. He saw other young girls carried on shoulders or lifted into arms. None of them were the girl he needed to find.

Nicolas wove back through the crowd, inspecting every vendor stand and game area. A flicker of orange caught his attention. Olive stood about thirty feet away, being led in the opposite direction by a woman. The girl had turned her head for a flash, and that had been enough time to capture his attention.

The woman was steering Olive to the outskirts of the park, holding her hand.

Breath rushed out of his lungs. He sprinted to them and cut off their route. His heart thudded against his ribs. "Olive. We've been looking all over for you." The person with Olive looked familiar, but he couldn't place her. He sent a quick message to Kayla, directing her to where they stood.

"Are you her father?" the woman asked him, pulling Olive closer.

"A friend of her sister." He didn't like the wariness in the woman's eyes. Then he remembered—she was an assistant to the director at the museum. Michelle was her name. "Kayla is coming."

"Well, I found this sweet little one wandering around all alone." Michelle didn't let go of Olive's hand. On the contrary, she seemed to increase her grip. "I was trying to find someone from law enforcement so I could report a missing child."

"Olive." Kayla exhaled a long breath as she ran up. She dropped onto her knees and pulled Olive in close, forcing Michelle to release her hold. "Thank goodness you're safe."

"Of course she is." Michelle reached over to brush the top of Olive's head with her hand. "You should keep a better eye on your sister."

"Where did you find her?" Nicolas asked.

"Over by the kettle corn stand." Gesturing toward the area, Michelle frowned. "She was almost in tears."

He searched Olive's face for any sign of distress. The face paint under her eyes was still crisp. She looked tired but not scared. Nicolas scooped her into his arms.

Olive dropped her head on his shoulder. "Hoppy," she mumbled, then placed a kiss on the stuffed animal's face.

"We're going home," Kayla announced. "Thank you for looking after her."

"Of course. She's only a little girl." Michelle's gaze rested on Olive, securely positioned up in his arms. "I won't hold who her father is against her."

Temper flashed in Kayla's eyes, and red patches appeared on her cheeks. She spun on her heel and marched away.

He hustled to keep up. A sleepy Olive was heavier than she looked.

"Don't let her get to you," he said to Kayla when they approached his vehicle.

"Easy for you to say." She made a sound of frustration. "You know what I was doing when I lost Olive? I was preoccupied by thinking about these people and how they're judging me. I cared so much about strangers' opinions that I wasn't paying attention to my sister."

"You're only human, Kayla." He said, attempting to soothe her. "Little kids pull disappearing acts all the time."

"But it's my job to protect her." Kayla shivered. "I failed because I can't get over the stigma of being associated with Trevor."

"She's safe." He opened the back door and placed Olive in her car seat. "Anyone who holds Trevor's actions against you isn't worthy of you. They don't know what a good person you are."

"Please take us home." Kayla climbed in the passenger's seat. She'd emotionally shut down and, in doing so, shut him out.

When he parked in the driveway to her mom's house, he hesitated, not knowing the right words to say.

"Th-thank you." Her voice cracked. "I'm sorry I got snippy. You found Olive and brought her back to me. I'm grateful."

"I would have turned over the entire town of Snowberry to find her. Do you want me to stay for a while?"

"No, but thanks. Detective Reimer instructed the on-duty deputies to monitor the house. It was great that you could spend the day with us." She pulled the door handle and slid out. "I'll keep in touch and let you know of any developments in the cases."

He didn't simply want to keep in touch. He didn't only want to know if something broke in either case. Nicolas wanted a chance to penetrate the thick walls around her. Though, would staying connected lead him to want more? Any relationship with Kayla other than a simple friendship was unsustainable.

While standing by his SUV, watching her go inside the house with Olive, he decided to call his mom and let her know he wouldn't be home tonight. He'd watch over Kayla and Olive all night long. Wherever they were, he'd be close by.

ELEVEN

Kayla's fingers hovered over her phone screen. She longed to text Nicolas or call him even. Plead for him to come back. Instead, she set her phone facedown on the table, then scrubbed her eyes. It wasn't late, but the day had sucked out all her energy. Those minutes when she couldn't find Olive had aged her years.

Steadfast Nicolas had come to the rescue, located her sister and placed her back with Kayla. She shouldn't have taken out her bad mood on him. Her irritation and frustration weren't his fault. History had a way of poking through the veil of time and finding the spots still tender. The reason she'd left Snowberry had been on display today at the park. Judgmental, small-minded people who made her feel vulnerable. She'd left for college without ridding herself of the chip on her shoulder. Even Nicolas remained in her line of fire.

Years ago, after the bar fight and his injury, she'd assumed he never wanted to speak with her again, and she avoided him. Her past with Nicolas had shored up her protective nature. *Don't put your faith in others and you won't get hurt.*

Kayla's mom shuffled into the kitchen and yawned. "Olive refuses to take a bath."

"She probably doesn't want her face paint washed off." Kayla pulled out a chair at the kitchen table. "Sit. You've been on your feet all day."

"My feet are fine." Even so, her mom dropped into the chair. "It's the rest of me crying out for rest."

"I'll tackle Olive and her bath." The teakettle on the stove whistled. Kayla poured hot water into a mug she'd placed a tea bag in earlier. Instead of taking the mug with her, she set it down on the table by her mom. "Take a moment to relax."

Before Kayla could walk away, her mom grasped her wrist. "Don't let pride keep you from calling Nicolas," she said. "It's not weakness to admit you need him."

"I don't want to ask too much of him. He should be with his family."

Her mom blew over the top of the mug, temporarily displacing the rising steam. "If he hadn't been with you at the park…"

"I know." Kayla raised her hands in a stop gesture. "I owe him so much already. The last thing I need is to add to my debt."

"Nicolas isn't keeping a tab."

"Maybe I am." Her foot tapped on the tile floor. "We're fine here in the house. On-duty deputies are driving by to check on us. Olive isn't wandering off again. Well, unless she really wants to avoid taking a bath." She sighed. "How about we watch a movie after bath time?"

"A nice relaxing activity that requires no physical effort. You got my vote."

Kayla left her mom sipping hot tea. She let Sasha outside to do her business and sniff around the yard. Next, she went into her bedroom to change into fleece pants and a comfy sweatshirt.

"No," Olive yelled from inside her bedroom down the hall. "I don't want a bath."

In the fenced-in backyard, Sasha barked. A request to be let inside after completing her business. She'd be fine out there for another minute or so. Otherwise, Kayla's mom could let her back in.

Closing her eyes, Kayla prayed for strength. She didn't have experience coercing a preschooler to do something she was dead set against. "After your bath, we'll watch a movie, and Ms. Hillary will make popcorn," she directed her voice to Olive's room. "How about that?" Her offer was met with silence.

A sharp breaking of glass shattered the quiet. Heart in her throat, Kayla turned to the direction of the noise. A chilly breeze flowed in through the hole that had been punched in her bedroom window, causing the curtain on her window to flutter. Her gaze dropped to the floor, where she found a rock laying on the carpet. A sheet of paper had been wrapped around the rock and secured by a rubber band. Kayla reached down to pick it up, then hesitated. Likely another threat. The rock and note were evidence. Best leave it for now.

She crept toward the window with nerves humming. The darkness outside was interrupted by the backyard security light. She could see a portion of the side yard.

By the rear of the fence, a figure disappeared into the shadows. *Get to your phone and call 911.*

Racing out of her room, she moved toward the kitchen. Olive's scream stopped her cold. Kayla darted into the room serving as Olive's bedroom, then shrieked. A person dressed in black and wearing a ski mask over their head was peering through the window. Same outfit as the person who'd attacked Kayla in Trevor's bathroom.

"Mom, call 911," she yelled at the top of her lungs.

At the sound of Kayla's voice, the person outside lowered out of sight.

She cautiously approached the window, checked the lock, then closed the blinds.

Sweeping Olive into her arms, she held on as if her sister would float away like a helium balloon if she let go.

"You're okay. You're safe." Kayla's words of comfort to Olive were meant for herself as well.

A knock sounded at the front door. Fear rushed through her veins. "Don't open it." Still holding on to Olive, she exited the bedroom.

"It's Nicolas," her mom called from the front of the house. The door banged shut followed by the click of the lock. "I called 911. What's going on?"

Kayla entered the living room.

Sasha lunged at them, sniffing up her leg to Olive. The dog whimpered.

"Someone threw a rock through my bedroom window. When I went into Olive's room, I saw a person lurking outside her window." She caught the tremble in her voice.

"Let me take Olive." Nicolas took two long strides and reached her.

She shook her head. Fear squeezed, making it hard to breathe.

"She's safe with me," he whispered and held out his hands. "Trust that I will protect her."

Kayla blinked. *Trust.* A belief she rarely afforded. She gazed into Nicolas's eyes. They shone with steadfast resolve. She handed over Olive and was met with a rush of immediate relief. Not only had Olive's physical weight been lifted but also some of her anxiety. He would protect Olive. Kayla trusted him with that responsibility.

"We're all safe." Kayla's mom kissed Olive's cheek.

Scenes flashed like a horror movie in her mind. "I couldn't ID the person." Her stomach roiled. "There was a note on the rock. I left it untouched in my bedroom."

Detective Reimer knocked on the door a few minutes later. She entered the room, and her focus immediately went to Olive, who sat snugly on Nicolas's lap while he read a story. "Tell me what happened."

Kayla reviewed the events that occurred only moments before. Part of Kayla's fear had transitioned into rage. "Let me show you the rock and note that were thrown through my bedroom window."

Detective Reimer followed her into the room and glanced around. She gloved her hands, then loosened the note from the rock.

Kayla read the note in the detective's hands.

Last warning. Place the jewels in the wood box in Trevor's backyard. Tell no one. You have twenty-four hours. If I don't have the jewels in my possession by tomorrow night, you, your sister and your mom will join Trevor.

The threat and deadline turned her stomach sick.

"Did you catch a look at the person?" Detective Reimer slipped the note into a clear evidence bag.

"I wish I had. Whoever they were was wearing a ski mask." More rage bubbled up. She needed a cool, rational head. She could lose it later.

"There are deputies searching the area and canvassing the neighborhood. If the person is still around, we'll find them."

"Who keeps harming my family? You must have some clues by now about who killed Trevor." Everything that happened since she arrived in Snowberry was connected. Of that she was sure.

Detective Reimer tapped her pen on the countertop. "I wish I had more news, Kayla."

"Detective," Kayla pleaded. "Olive and I will die if you don't stop these people. Trevor had asked me to give something to federal law enforcement, not the Temple County Sheriff's Department." Could she trust Detective Reimer? Until now, she'd trusted them to protect her family because she'd had no choice. "Do you know if Trevor was working with anyone outside your department? Maybe as an informant?"

"We've known each other since our school days, so please call me Christina." She rested a hand on Kayla's shoulder. "I'm working some strong leads and have been in contact with the Salt Lake City FBI Office. And yes, between you and me, several of those leads have taken me in some disturbing directions. I'll tell you more as soon as I have definitive information. Right now, I think you should move your family to a different location. Somewhere others won't know to look for you."

"I'll take Olive and my mom home to Colorado Springs." Her condo wasn't set up for three people and a dog, but they'd make it work. "We can leave tonight."

"You'll need to find somewhere closer than Colorado Springs." Opening the weather app on her phone, Christina pulled up the alert. "The nice weather we had today is being followed by a cold front. They're predicting one of the worst snowstorms in years. You'll never make it through the mountains if you head south."

Kayla read the script highlighted in red. A severe winter storm warning had been issued. Snow was predicted to begin at midnight. At least a foot was expected with blowing and drifting, making travel hazardous. "It's April and the temps today were in the sixties."

"The weather here doesn't always abide by the calendar. Do you have somewhere closer where you can hide out for a while?"

Kayla's mom stepped into the kitchen. "Becky's cabin. She's a friend I've had since childhood. It's about sixty miles west of town. I'm sure she'd let us stay there if I asked. If we hurry, we can be there before the snow starts."

Her gut clenched at the prospect of driving through a snowstorm. "Are you sure it's a good idea to leave?"

What was the alternative though? Stay and remain a target. As long as Trevor's killer was still on the loose and they believed she had the stolen necklace and diamonds, all of them had a giant flashing target on their backs.

"I do," Christina said. "You should start packing. We'll set up surveillance on Trevor's backyard with the hope that whoever is threatening you will show, and we can end this once and for all."

Kayla stared at her mom. How could this be happening? "I'm scared."

Her mom sighed. "I am too. We'll stick together. There's no way I'm letting either one of you out of my sight."

"Same." Nicolas strode up to Kayla. His tall posture and broad shoulders left no room for disagreement.

Yet, as always, Kayla tried. "Nicolas, are you sure?"

"I've never been more sure of anything." His nostrils flared. "I was outside in my car when I heard your scream. I stayed, watching the house. And I failed because whoever threw the rock slipped past me. I won't let that happen again."

Her next statement was cut off as she considered what he'd just said. Instead of going home, he'd watched the house. Nicolas had been here moments after she noticed the intruder. "You're not responsible for us." Her tone lacked fight.

"If not me, then who?" The corner of his mouth lifted, exposing one dimple. "Accept it, Swartz, you're stuck with me."

How was she managing to smile? After all the bad, Nicolas kept a light burning in her soul. Kayla pressed her lips together. "Fine, you can come. Only because Olive adores you."

"I adore her." His gaze fixed on Kayla. "When this is over, you owe me a visit. Southern Cali is beautiful in the late spring."

"A trip to the beach someday sounds wonderful." The fantasy brought with it a reminder his real life was far away.

"I have a go-bag in my SUV. I'm ready whenever you are." He strode over to the window facing the front lawn and stood monitoring the activity outside.

Kayla turned to Olive on the sofa and observed her for a minute.

Olive pointed to a picture in a book. Hoppy stayed propped at the girl's side. Her sister appeared calm and comfortable.

Kayla's rapidly beating heart slowed. Olive would be kept safe until the bad people were caught. She found her mom in the kitchen. "We have a lot to pack."

"I know. We'll still have a nice Easter meal. We'll still be together to celebrate." Kayla's mom took out paper grocery bags from the cupboard and handed two to her.

They'd be together. Trevor would be absent. Nicolas would help fill the void. While packing Sasha's food and other items she'd need, Kayla prayed to God for continued protection. She prayed for Olive and that her, her mom's and Nicolas's love for the little girl would overshadow the trauma she had experienced in her short life. She prayed for Christina and the other members of law enforcement working to bring Trevor's killer to justice. And she prayed for Nicolas and thanked God for second chances. For Trevor, his second chance at redemption was cut short.

Christina left with little new information. She asked Kayla to contact her once they arrived at the cabin.

Within an hour, Nicolas's SUV and her mom's truck were packed tightly. An ice-cold wind swept in like a herald of bad tidings.

Seated in the passenger seat of Nicolas's SUV, Kayla glanced back at her mom's house. It was soon swallowed up in the darkness.

TWELVE

A light snow started as soon as Nicolas got up into the mountains. Christina was right. With a possible blizzard blowing in from the west to hit Montana and Wyoming overnight, they wouldn't have made it out of the state. He would have followed them anywhere, but keeping closer to Snowberry made returning to his regular life easier once this situation was over. Taking Kayla, Hillary and Olive to a cabin was smart. As the cabin had no direct connection to any of them, they'd be kept hidden and away from danger until the perpetrators were caught.

He had a handgun locked in a case stashed far in the glove box. Hillary thought the owner of the cabin had rifles for hunting stored there in a safe. He didn't expect trouble, but having some firepower at his disposal provided comfort.

Nicolas checked the rearview mirror. Hillary followed close behind. Headlights bounced off the trees lining the road. Between people, pets, clothing and food, his SUV wasn't large enough to fit it all. He sat beside Kayla, with Olive and Sasha in the back seat.

He increased his grip on the steering wheel at a series of switchback turns. Each mile brought them higher in elevation. In the stillness of the vehicle with the radio playing soft music, he considered his choices since arriving in Snowberry. He'd always jumped in first and thought about the effects later. After he told Kayla he was coming with them to the cabin, he had a short moment of doubt. His obligation was to his business back home. He had planned to fly back in two days. Unless the people threatening Kayla and Olive were caught tomorrow, his trip home would be delayed. Before leaving, he'd called his partner to discuss upcoming assignments. His job was to protect others. No one needed his protection more than the people riding with him.

By the time he pulled into the driveway of the cabin, the digital clock on the dash read 11:00 p.m.

Hillary parked her truck beside his SUV. Both vehicles faced the dark cabin. Olive stirred in the back seat, having dozed off during the ride.

He yawned and exited the SUV, then looked at Kayla. "You get Olive inside and settled, and I'll start hauling in stuff."

"You mean my mom's entire kitchen, including the sink?" Kayla grinned. "There is no packing light with this group."

"I'd carry four times this amount to earn a spot at her table for Easter dinner." Guilt poked at missing his own family's celebration. He promised himself he'd make it up to them. He strode to the rear of the SUV and lifted the door. Olive's duffle bag tumbled onto the ground.

Lifting it, he was surprised at its weight. "I think I found the kitchen sink."

Carrying Olive, Kayla glanced at the bulging bag. "She couldn't leave behind any of her dolls. I'm thankful she didn't insist on bringing the play kitchen and every stuffed animal."

"She has her bunny, I see." His heart warmed at the sight of Olive snug against Kayla with the purple bunny tucked in her arms.

"Of course." Kayla pressed a kiss on the girl's forehead. "It's colder up here. I'll bring her inside."

Hillary had unlocked the door and flipped on some interior lights. The cabin glowed warm and welcoming.

His instincts brought him here. If all remained quiet during their time at the cabin, he wouldn't regret coming. He hoped that they would enjoy a relaxing break from fear and grief and that he'd have the opportunity to reconnect with Kayla before he'd have to let her go again.

Kayla awoke with a start. Her heart thudded. The dream that had haunted her sleep finally dissipated like fog on a fall morning. She moved up to sit in bed, careful not to wake Olive, who snoozed on the other side.

Sasha rested on her cushion on the floor. The dog glanced at her with hooded eyes, found Olive still tucked in and lowered her head again.

Curtains covered the windows, but some daylight spilled in. She checked the time—well past her normal alarm clock setting. They'd all had a late night. Sliding her legs out from under the covers, she sucked in a breath. Gooseflesh pricked on her bare skin. *Brrr.* First order of business was to stoke the fire in the hearth.

Kayla changed into sweatpants and a hoodie. On the way past the mirror, she checked her reflection. The bags under her eyes didn't enhance her appearance. Her brunette locks tumbled over her shoulders. She shrugged. Her vanity would be locked away for the foreseeable future. Once she was sure of their safety, she could worry about her looks again.

With Olive still sleeping, Kayla gently closed the door behind her. She tiptoed down the hallway, then froze at the view in the living room. It wasn't the picturesque scene out the front window that captured her attention. Nicolas lay on the sofa, stretched out with his feet propped up and over its edge. A blanket covered his sizeable form. She took a moment to watch him sleep. The man who seemed invincible while awake appeared childlike in slumber.

He'd insisted on sleeping on the sofa last night, even though Kayla had offered to share a bed with her mom and Olive to leave the second bedroom for him. Nicolas wanted to be out in the open in case someone broke in. The front door and windows had security bars, mostly to defend against wildlife invaders but were effective against the human kind too. He would be the first line of defense. Of course, she'd countered that sleeping on the sofa would make him more tired and less aware during the day. Her argument struck closed ears.

She added a log to the smoldering fire, then left him to his dreams. Next stop was the kitchen to start the coffee. Soon, the rich aroma stirred Nicolas and her mom. Both of them shuffled into the kitchen and fumbled around the cabinets until the mugs were located.

"Good morning," Kayla said over the lip of her full coffee mug. First up claimed first pour.

"Morning." Nicolas rubbed his eyes. "It was a quiet night."

"The nearest cabin is several miles away," her mom said while pouring. "I pray that the only sounds we hear are those of nature and one another."

"Cheers to that." Kayla held up her mug, then took another drink. "I feel bad for missing Easter service this morning. Do you think we can stream it on TV?"

Kayla's mom glanced outside. The terrain was covered in white. Snowflakes drifted down at a relentless pace. The sharp wind whipped past the window pane. "Depends on if the internet works."

Kayla checked the service on her cell phone. Nothing. Not surprising. Service at any mountainous area was spotty, and bad weather interfered with any signal that normally reached those areas. Christina had given her a satellite phone before leaving, and Kayla had used it to contact her last night after they'd arrived. The satellite phone might not work with the now heavy cloud cover, but the device served as a communication option.

"We can at least start breakfast. That is, if the stove works." The antique cast-iron beast stared at her in a challenge.

"I'll worry about breakfast," her mom said. "I brought ingredients for pancakes, if that's all right with everyone. How about you two work on getting that fire roaring again?"

"Yes, ma'am. Pancakes for a fire is a fine deal." Mug in hand, Nicolas left the kitchen to deal with the fireplace.

Kayla followed him. She reclined in one of the large upholstered chairs and watched him work. He added to the one log she'd placed inside earlier. Soon, flames danced and offered a welcome warmth. "I hope we can make a nice Easter for Olive. With the snow, I assume a colored egg hunt outside is off the agenda."

"Easter will be special. Olive is with you and your mom. That's all that matters." Nicolas set another log on the fire before sitting on the floor by the hearth.

"And you," Kayla added. "My sister thinks you're the bee's knees."

He chuckled. "I never understood what that expression meant."

It means you are simply perfect. "Olive likes you. She feels safe with you. You're really good with her. Maybe you should switch careers from a bodyguard to a preschool teacher."

"Sure, but only if I can be like Arnold in *Kindergarten Cop*," he spoke in a pretend Austrian accent. "I enjoy my profession. I considered joining the Secret Service when my military service was complete, but the idea of owning my own business grew too hard to resist."

"Do you have many celebrity clients? Anyone I might know?" She pictured him spending countless hours around beautiful women. A spike of jealousy pricked her.

"My company handles protection services for many celebrities. The perks of being the boss is I can select which ones I want to work with." He grinned, showing his dimples. "But the disadvantage of being the boss is that I deal with any problematic clients, and most of those are famous and extremely rich."

How could she—Kayla Swartz, art teacher, therapy dog handler and now single parent to a young girl—compete with all that glitz and glamour? Reality dampened some of her joy over being with Nicolas again. He loved his work and being his own boss. Their worlds would never fit together.

"What about you?" He nudged her.

"Teaching kindergarten might be a nice change of pace after dealing with teenagers for five years."

"I can imagine. But I mean, what do you think about me? Do you consider me the bee's knees too?" He arched a black eyebrow.

Her mouth went dry. Another drink of coffee did not provide relief. Kayla couldn't admit her true feelings. His life was big and bold and located in Los Angeles. Hers was the opposite. "You're a good friend, missing your family Easter celebration to help us." She swallowed hard. "I feel better knowing you're here."

He broke eye contact and glanced at the flat-screen TV set on a stand. "I'll see if the internet is working so we can watch the Easter service." Nicolas spent the next few minutes pressing buttons on the remote.

She savored the moment, tucked away in a mountain cabin with a fire burning in the hearth. The weather had only worsened overnight. A spring blizzard was what the weather report called it. In her opinion, blizzards and spring didn't mix. The good thing about these late-season snowstorms was the assurance all the snow and ice wouldn't hang around long. Spring bulbs that had started poking out their shoots from the cold ground would find the sun again. They'd grow and bloom, sprinkling the dull-colored earth with pops of yellow, purple, red and green.

Checking on Nicolas's progress, she noted a frozen image of the interior of their church on the TV screen. "It's a start."

"The internet is weak. We don't have enough bandwidth for streaming." He flicked off the TV and tossed the remote on the stand. "Honestly, I'm surprised we have internet at all. My cell phone isn't getting service."

She checked her phone again, no bars. A hit of panic propelled her over to the landline phone secured to the wall. Lifting the receiver, she calmed at the sound of a dial tone. She'd lived through Montana storms when phone service and electricity were knocked out.

She should call Christina and check in. While inhaling the delicious scents of pancakes cooking on the griddle, she took out the detective's business card and powered up the satellite phone. After walking around the cabin without getting a signal due to the heavy cloud cover outside, she made the call on the landline. Their conversation was brief. Christina provided an update on the progress of the cases. They were looking into Paula and her boyfriend, Sam Porter, along with a list of others. Nothing solid so far. Not enough to make an arrest.

Kayla considered the possibility, debating if Trevor would be a party to a crime in order to protect Olive. Paula had lost her parental rights a year ago. Even so, she might threaten to make Trevor and Olive's lives unpleasant if she didn't get her way.

The call ended just in time for the announcement that breakfast was ready. In a flash, Olive and Sasha appeared from the bedroom, looking fully rested and ready to eat.

Kayla let out Sasha, then fed her.

The dog seemed unimpressed with her kibble but ate it anyway. Her full tummy didn't stop her from begging for bits of Olive's syrupy pancake from the table. For her part, Olive obliged, seeming to not want her new best friend to miss out on yummy people food.

With the batch of pancakes wiped out, mostly thanks to Nicolas, Kayla collected dishes, then started cleaning up. Preparation for the Easter meal would start soon. Using history as her guide, Kayla would likely be banned from the kitchen due to her propensity to burn food she was charged with cooking. Dishwashing duty was fine with her. Nothing to turn to charcoal in a sink full of soapy water.

Nicolas had gotten out the carton of hardboiled eggs from the refrigerator and began preparing cups of dye. He stayed focused as he went about his tasks. Guess they took Easter egg dyeing seriously in the Galanis house.

Catching sight of Olive playing dolls in the living room, Kayla called her mom over. "I spoke with Detective Reimer. She has Olive's mom on her suspect list."

Kayla's mom picked up a towel and began drying dishes on the rack. "I hope that's not the case. My heart would break if Paula had killed Trevor or if he'd been killed under her orders. That would be an extra cruel burden for Olive."

"I agree. I remember when Olive came to live with Trevor." Concern about her father being primary caregiver to a toddler had propelled her north to check in. What she found had surprised her. Trevor had acted like a committed, responsible father. When Kayla had expressed her concern to her mom, she had assured Kayla that she'd keep an eye on the situation. Olive deserved a stable life despite her parents' foolishness. "He was convinced Olive was his second chance to get things right."

"Trevor wanted to mend things with you." Kayla's mom swept a lock of hair off her cheek.

Speaking of him in the past tense pierced her heart. She shook off the feeling, not strong enough to carry the weight of grief right now. Once his killer was caught and locked behind bars, maybe then she'd sit with her emotions.

"Trevor left me as Olive's guardian in his will." She'd made the decision to accept his wishes and file for legal custody. "I wonder if Paula has family who may step forward and fight me."

Hillary shook her head. "Not that I know of. Trevor never mentioned any of Paula's kin wanting to see Olive after she came to live with him."

Good. Better to have one sister who loved the child to the moon and back than a large family filled with dysfunction. "What if Olive's mom is behind this? If Paula takes Olive, she gets her daughter back and quiets a potential witness." The suggestion made her sick. The pancakes she'd consumed less than an hour ago sat heavy in her gut. As she had time to consider the possibility, the more it made sense. A deep criminal history mixed with vengeance and greed were strong incentives.

"No matter who is responsible, we will do anything to protect Olive." Dishcloth abandoned on the rack, her mom opened the refrigerator and pulled out ingredients for their next meal. Soon, various types of cheese, milk, potatoes, ham, green beans and premade bread dough covered the countertop.

Kayla wanted to share her mom's confidence. After the horrors they'd experienced over the last few days, she wouldn't assume anywhere was safe.

She took down her contribution to dinner from the top of the fridge—a store-bought iced lemon cake. Once the dishes were cleaned and put away, Kayla was gently removed from the kitchen.

In contrast, Nicolas was invited in, handed an apron and given the recipe for scalloped potatoes.

Fine. Let Nicolas cook while I play with Olive and Sasha. It wasn't her fault she had issues operating a stove.

While the meal cooked, Nicolas took out a Bible he'd found on one of the shelves in the living room. He flipped through the pages until he found the section he wanted.

Kayla curled up on the sofa with Olive and Sasha, and listened to Nicolas read from Psalms, a message filled with love and hope. His deep voice soothed her, inviting a peace she hadn't experienced since receiving the panicked call from Trevor.

She could get used to cuddles after a long day of

work. The reality of raising a child and all the hard work that came with it only briefly occupied her mind. Moments like this one would make the struggles worthwhile.

As Nicolas finished the reading, he met Kayla's gaze. Each day together intensified their bond. She would hurt, like yanking out stitches, when the time came for them to part ways for good.

THIRTEEN

Nicolas tucked the Bible back onto the shelf. His parents likely were upset he wasn't sitting next to them in the pew this morning. They hadn't been thrilled he remained with Kayla even though they understood his reasons. His life in LA wasn't conducive to his faith. Ever since leaving Snowberry for the military, he'd felt the war in his soul. Reading the words of the Bible while Kayla, Olive and Hillary listened reminded him that he'd let his relationship with God starve for too long. For years, he'd fought against acknowledging the hole in his life. Money and success didn't completely fulfill him. Deep down, he knew he needed more.

Hillary returned to the kitchen, Olive in tow, with the promise of helping make the deviled eggs. She'd won Olive's attention for the short term.

"I overheard you mention Olive's mom and her boyfriend are suspects." Too restless to sit, he added another log on the fire. "Did Christina mention if they're close to an arrest?"

"She didn't say. The last time she mentioned them,

Paula and Sam were on the run." Kayla glanced outside at a world covered in white. "My gut tells me they're not involved. I can't believe Olive's mom killed her daughter's father in cold blood."

He considered the boyfriend and assumed his ethics might not rise to the level of protecting his girlfriend's ex. While studying war and human nature, he'd learned people were capable of defending the indefensible, as long as it suited their purpose. "They'll get the guilty parties."

"I'm glad you're so confident." Reclining on the sofa, she pulled a blanket over her lap. "I'm sure there is pressure to find the museum thief and retrieve the goods. Sheriff Gomez didn't act concerned about finding Trevor's murderer. Then again, Trevor was not one of Snowberry's more respected citizens."

"He's a victim and deserves justice as much as anyone else." Nicolas agreed with Kayla's point. The Snowberry community wasn't a metropolitan area with a large police force. Rural towns tended to operate differently. Residents labeled bad had a hard time removing the tag. If someone was arrested or, worse yet, convicted of a crime, everyone knew within a few days.

"When I was a girl, I dreaded going to Trevor's house for visits. My mom tried making it seem like a fun trip, but I saw the worry in her eyes." She sniffled. "By the time I got to high school, I rarely saw him. After that night at the bar when you got hurt, I swore I'd never speak to him again."

Regret poured in. "I shouldn't have blamed him or you. I'm sorry for acting that way."

She held up her hands. "You should have played football in college and professionally. You would have if not for the injury."

Back then, he'd considered her more than a friend. "I think it's time we move on from that time in our lives. I have no regrets over the way my life turned out." With one exception—the loss of Kayla in his life for so many years.

"I'll let go of old guilt if you can. You'd be successful no matter what obstacles were tossed in your way." A melancholy smile lifted her lips. "You're a fighter, so of course you make a great bodyguard."

Concerns about his business came and went. His house near the beach in Malibu seemed a half a world away. A long string of texts from his partner prodded his mind about work responsibilities. Their newest client would arrive on Tuesday. Nicolas had done his best to manage from out of town. Once he returned home, he'd need to jump back into business tasks without hesitation.

"Underneath my expensive work suit," he said, "I'm a Montana boy at heart."

Her smile brightened her face and sparkled in her blue eyes. "I'd like to see you on the job." Her eyebrows waggled. "Do you wear dark sunglasses and never smile like the Secret Service?"

"I never smile while on the job, and the sunglasses shield my eyes for the camera flashes. I don't look as uptight as the Secret Service. They have that guise down to an art form." His cheeks warmed under her admiring stare. Memories of their young romance burst like fireworks. For a time, he'd believed Kayla was the one. Looking at her now, he wondered if she always had been. No woman he'd dated touched his heart like Kayla did. No one challenged him like Kayla or caused him to question his path in life.

A gust of wind rattled the windows in their panes. The view of the lake, which rested a few hundred feet out the front door, lay veiled in blowing snow. As long as they had wood for the fire and each other for company, he didn't want to be anywhere else.

Olive ran into the room, arms outstretched to Nicolas. "When do I find eggs?"

Kayla stared outside. "I don't think we can do an Easter egg hunt outside. We can hide some around the cabin. You also have an Easter basket to find."

"Yes!" Olive hopped onto the sofa and began jumping. "Teddy bear."

Nicolas followed to where Olive's finger pointed. Had she dropped one of her stuffed animals on the way in last night? If so, the poor thing would be buried in snow by now.

"All your teddy bears are over there." Kayla pointed to the colorful pile of stuffed animals in the corner of the room.

"Teddy bear." Olive leaned forward until her forehead pressed onto the glass.

"Come here." Nicolas lifted her off the sofa, then spun her around in a circle. "How about you go in your bedroom so Kayla can hide the eggs and your basket? You can pick out a book for me to read."

Teddy bear forgotten, Olive raced to the room she shared with Kayla.

"You're a magician," Kayla declared. "How do you feel about adding babysitting to your bodyguard duties?"

"Only for Olive." He couldn't imagine not being a part of their lives. Not after everything they'd been through together. How would he balance work with traveling to visit Kayla?

A loud bang sounded, followed by another. Someone or something was outside.

"Stay back." He waved Kayla away from the window while creeping forward. When noise that sounded closer to a crash burst forth, he darted behind the curtain. The window covering was pushed to the side, offering little cover.

I need my gun. Nicolas raced into the kitchen, then removed the gun case on the top shelf in one of the wall cabinets. Using the key stored in his jeans pocket, he opened the lid and checked the weapon. He'd kept the gun loaded in case he needed it in a hurry. "Make sure Olive stays in her room." He did not want the child anywhere near him while he handled a firearm.

Kayla nodded, taking position in the entryway between the living room and hallway.

More noise outside. Whoever was out there wasn't hiding their presence.

He unlocked the front door. With controlled movements, he opened the door and peered out. He could see nothing other than snow and trees. Holding his gun at the ready, he stepped onto the porch. His gaze swept the area, and his heart leaped at the hulking form only a dozen feet away. Olive's teddy bear was better known around the Rocky Mountains as a grizzly. Relief and terror hit at once.

The formidable beast rose up on its hind legs and sniffed the air. A panting sound mixed with a low growl pierced the air.

Nicolas froze on his spot on the porch. Behind his back, he waved at Kayla to stay inside. The gun in his hand provided a reassuring weight. Not that a handgun would stop a six-hundred-pound bear, but a bullet or two aimed in the right spot would slow it down. Though he'd rather not hurt or kill this magnificent creature. As long as each minded its own business, they'd go their separate ways in peace.

"Olive's right. It does look like a teddy bear," Kayla whispered from behind. "How can it be dangerous with those cute little ears?"

He almost laughed. "Get closer and some of the cuteness is traded for killer claws and teeth." His voice remained hushed.

The bear glanced in the direction of the cabin. Its interested seemed to peak at the sight of them.

Great. He stepped forward and pointed his gun in the air. The blast might scare it off. Once clear from the porch overhang, he fired one shot, earning only a brief flinch from the bear.

"Right behind you," Hillary announced. "Don't shoot again." Were those pots in her hands?

Hillary banged together the bottom of two steel pots, making enough noise to wake the dead. "Scat. Be gone with you. You'll find nothing to munch on here." More banging.

With a perturbed sounding grunt, the bear shook its head then lumbered off into the woods at the shoreline of the lake.

Hillary took the rifle she'd placed by her feet, wrapped her hands around the stock, and pointed the muzzle at the ground. "Glad the big guy took the hint. I didn't want to use this." She flicked a glance at the rifle and grinned. "Yes, I know how to shoot. My daddy taught me to hunt in these mountains around the same time I learned how to read."

"The Montana way." He held open the door for Hillary, then followed her inside. Another thing he missed about his home state. He'd learned to live off the land and hunt for food. People here respected nature and, for the most part, worked to protect it. A lot of people grew their own food using greenhouses for year-round fresh vegetables. His heart yearned for a clear river, a fly-fishing pole and an entire day to spend in the wild—free of car horns, jet engines and other people. On second thought, there was one person's company he'd gladly welcome.

Kayla locked the door behind him, finally able to breathe normally. "It's a good thing we didn't hunt for eggs outside." She waited until the guns were locked and put away before getting Olive.

The moment the door to the bedroom opened, Olive darted out and bounded onto the sofa. "Where's the teddy bear?"

Kayla suppressed a laugh since Olive appeared stricken. "He went to find his family. They're having a special meal for Easter too."

"Oh." Olive glanced out the window, searching the yard. "Where's my basket?"

How she envied the ease at which children moved on from disappointment. "You go into the kitchen with Ms. Hillary, and Nicolas and I will hide your basket and the eggs. We'll let you know when it's time to find them."

Olive peered at Kayla like she was debating whether to cooperate or not. "Okay," she finally said. Her small hand grasped in Kayla's mom's, the two walked into the kitchen with a promise of jelly beans.

"Don't spoil her appetite," Kayla called out after them.

"Your mom won't let her overdo it." Nicolas stood behind her, too close.

His breath warmed the back of her neck. Her flannel shirt felt overly thick, and she rolled up her sleeves. "Do you mind helping to hide them?"

"Of course not. I wish I had an Easter bunny costume."

"I'm glad you don't." She didn't want to have the image of tall, muscular Nicolas dressed as a pastel bunny burned into her memory. The way he looked— worn jeans, off-white sweater and ruffled dark hair with a scruffy dark beard—was flawless in her eyes.

When the basket and colored eggs were hidden, Olive burst out of the kitchen in a sugar rush and tore around the interior of the cabin. She didn't take long to find her basket and all but one egg, which neither Kayla nor Nicolas could remember where they'd placed.

She'd find it before leaving, or the cabin's owner would discover a rotten surprise some day.

They ate a large meal around the table. Kayla savored the moment. As horrible as her visit to Snowberry had been, this time with Olive, her mom and Nicolas soothed her. In the days to come, she'd say goodbye to Nicolas, but no distance between them would erase these memories.

At last, with dishes done and Olive passed out on the sofa, Kayla tidied up. *Enjoy it now. The moment you get word the people threatening you and Olive are caught, you'll pack up and head home.*

Several of Olive's dolls were scattered on the living room floor. Kayla found Olive's duffle bag and opened it. As she set the first of many dolls inside the bag, a quick glance brought her attention to the corner of a manila envelope. The eight-by-ten envelope was tucked underneath the stiff removable bottom of the bag. Taking out the envelope, she studied the plain exterior. Had Trevor placed it inside or someone else?

Kayla lifted the top flap then extracted a stack of photocopied pages. *What is this?* She peeked in the envelope again to make sure she didn't miss anything. A plain half sheet of paper remained stuffed at the bottom. When she pulled it out and saw her name scrolled in her father's handwriting, her heart stopped.

Kayla. These are copies from an accounting ledger. Take them to the FBI. The guilty must answer for their crimes.

What had possessed her father to hide evidence of crimes in Olive's duffle bag? The answer jolted her heart—the hiding place was meant to be short term. Trevor had expected to hand it over to Kayla at the motel. He hadn't expected to be murdered.

FOURTEEN

Seated at the table, Kayla flipped through the pages. "These are copies of someone's accounting records."

"Whose though?" Nicolas leaned forward to get a closer look.

She kept her voice low. Her mom had taken Olive into the bedroom for nap time. A treat Kayla wished she could take advantage of. And she would have enjoyed a moment of rest if not for this latest discovery. Each page was neatly laid out with dates, dollar amounts and names. None of the names appeared genuine. Whoever the ledger belonged to used pseudonyms to keep those related to the numbers a secret.

Kayla ran her finger across a page, moving from name to date to dollar amount and ending with another figure. "My guess is this belongs to someone with an under-the-table loan business."

Nicolas flipped back to the first page. "Here's a reference to an MT. Who might that be?"

She considered the possibilities. "The only person I know with those initials who associated with my dad is Manny Tarin. There's more writing at the bottom of the last page, almost too light to read." She'd missed it at first glance. "Tijuana, Juárez and a list of names under each heading."

"I'd like to go back in time and ask Trevor," Nicolas said. "You may be right about Trevor working as an informant."

"If that were the case, all the secrecy makes sense. Even Trevor's request not to hand over what he had to the Temple County Sheriff's Department." She rested her head in her hands. "I trust Christina, though. I hate to bother her on Easter, but if this information can lead to Trevor's murderer, then she'll want to be updated right away."

Bad weather often interrupted cell service, landlines, satellite signals and the power supply. Their electricity hadn't gone out, so hope remained the landline was still operational. But just because it wasn't down here didn't mean the lines were standing in town. The heavy snow would coat tree branches. Often those branches would break and land on utility lines and other things.

She lifted the old-school phone receiver and heard a static dial tone. The satellite phone signal continued to be blocked by bad weather. After dialing Christina's number, she stretched the phone cord until she stood at the table. Disappointment hit when a voicemail recording played. Kayla left a brief message. Nothing more to do than wait for a return call. The roads would be dangerous to travel.

A minute after she hung up the phone, it rang. The burst of noise in the otherwise quiet house made her jump. "Hello," she answered.

"Kayla, it's Christina. I got your message. Tell me what you found." The sound of her voice cut in and out.

"Trevor hid some copied pages in Olive's duffle bag. I think it's from an accounting ledger." She returned to the table and reviewed the pages. "Most of the names listed beside dollar amounts and dates are those of celebrities or fictional characters. On the back page, someone wrote down the names of several cities in Mexico with long column numbers and names recorded below each."

"Does it say who the accounting information belonged to?" Christina said.

Kayla hesitated. Had she put them in more danger by telling Christina what she'd found? She'd keep the faith in the only person who'd shown an effort to solve Trevor's murder. "There are initials listed on the first page, which might be for Manny Tarin." If the accounting ledger tied Manny to criminal activity, why and how did Trevor come to possess a copy? A prolonged silenced filled the line, and Kayla worried the call had been cut off.

"I've had suspicion for some time that Manny and his crew were trafficking drugs and laundering money for a Mexican cartel," Christina finally said. "A former Temple County Deputy, Marcus Gray, was convicted of suppressing evidence. Trevor testified against him. I believe Gray had ties to Manny's operation, but we couldn't prove the connection. Until now."

"How?" Kayla asked. Had Trevor's death been due to his attempt to provide evidence about Manny's operation? Was it tied to the museum theft? Or both?

"Marcus Gray was found shot and killed this afternoon. Manny fled Gray's house after gunfire was heard. We've been unable to locate Manny."

"Do you believe Manny killed Trevor? Is he the one behind the mailbox bomb and attempt to kidnap Olive?" Her thoughts turned to her sister. *Please, God, continue to keep her safe.*

"I don't know for sure, but recent events point in his direction." The phone line buzzed with static, then Christina's voice reemerged. "…cartel."

"You cut out at the end. What about the cartel?" Kayla strained to hear every word.

"My suspicion is Manny used cartel money for making loans. Once the accounting ledger is examined, we can start piecing together all the connections," Christina said. "I assume the cartel didn't know about Manny's side hustle. If he lost some of their money, he'd be desperate to make up the amount.

"Desperate enough to steal valuable jewelry and diamonds from the museum? Desperate enough to kill to get it back?" Her body chilled. If Manny had the stolen valuables, she wouldn't have found him drinking beers at Big Sky Tavern the other day. She thought back to their encounter. Manny had appeared relaxed, not concerned about anything other than getting his hands on the jewels. As deeply as Kayla wanted to trust Trevor's rehabilitation from crime, indications were that he'd been involved in the heist.

"There's an APB for Manny and several men he's known to associate with. As of now, I don't know if he's still in the area or has fled."

"What if he learns where we're hiding?" Anger at her father burned through her. If Trevor had the necklace and diamonds, why not hand them over immediately? He likely would have been arrested on suspicion of theft but better that than his daughters becoming the target of an assassin.

"Keep calm," Christina said, attempting to reassure her. "Does Manny have any knowledge about your connection to your mom's friend who owns the cabin?"

"I don't believe so. My mom steered clear of those men." Kayla pressed a hand to her heart, attempting to calm her heart rate.

"As soon as the roads are clear, I'll drive to the cabin and check in. Utility poles and trees have been knocked down by the storm. The snow and ice are making the roads unmanageable."

"Please be in touch if you learn anything more." As long as the phones worked.

"Will do. And Kayla, hide that ledger. It's a crucial piece of evidence we need to tie all these loose strings together. Take some pictures of the pages just in case the photocopies get damaged between now and when we can collect it for evidence."

When the call ended, Kayla sank onto a chair and met Nicolas's gaze. "The deputy Trevor testified against is dead. They think Manny shot him and is on the run." She slid the stack of papers across the table to rest in front of Nicolas. "The theory is that this is an accounting of illegal loans made with drug cartel money. Christina thinks Manny was running a side hustle without the cartel's blessing."

"Working for the cartel isn't smart, but embezzling from them is really dumb." Nicolas flipped through the pages again. "How does Trevor fit into all this?"

She shrugged. "You and my mom believed he'd changed, and I'd like to believe that too. I've distrusted him my entire life, and my soul is weary from carrying the burden."

Nicolas straightened the papers, then stood. While pouring two mugs of coffee, he looked out the kitchen window. "What if he was trying to make things right? Trevor had gone to Manny a few weeks ago, asking for work. Maybe the request was a cover to gain access to that." Nicolas pointed at the photocopies. "Our responsibility is not to solve the crime but to stay safe."

"Stay safe from the giant mess left in Trevor's wake." Kayla accepted the warm mug Nicolas handed over. She flipped through memories of her childhood when jealousy had overwhelmed her. She'd imagined the fathers of her friends as her own. Those fathers didn't drink too much or fight with people at the house when she was around. Those fathers read bedtime stories and tucked their little girls into bed at the end of the day. Those fathers were good and cared about their children more than they did everything else. She'd prayed to God to give her a good father—one she wasn't embarrassed of.

When she grew old enough, she started a new life away from Trevor. And now, her father was gone. Forever. Young Kayla wouldn't understand her current grief over his death. She'd reminded her adult self of how Trevor had only ever brought pain and sadness into her life, and this current situation was a prime example.

Olive and Sasha tumbled into the kitchen. The curly haired girl and fluffy dog appeared to morph into one as they wandered the room searching the countertops for something good to eat.

Kayla watched Olive stretch up on tiptoes and reach toward the bag of jelly beans tucked back against the tile backsplash. Sasha stared up at her friend with expectation in her big brown eyes.

"Hold on." She hustled over before Olive got ahold of the bag of candy. "I'll make you a snack. Something with a little less sugar."

The scowl Olive sent Kayla lifted her spirits.

"You used to make that same face when you didn't get your way, as I remember," Kayla's mom said as she entered. "Still do, now that I think of it."

Smiling, Kayla opened the cabinet and took out the loaf of bread. She'd admit that Trevor had brought more to her life than pain and sadness. He'd trusted her with Olive. No matter if Trevor was innocent or guilty, Kayla would have the blessing of her sister.

A steely twilight rested over the landscape outside the cabin. Nicolas had gone out to grab some more wood to bring inside. A large pile of split wood was stacked on a covered rack at the rear of the cabin. Feeling restless, he found an axe and some logs. They had plenty of dry wood already, but he needed to burn some energy. He wasn't used to being confined inside for long periods of time. Not that being sequestered with Kayla was a bad thing. If the circumstances were less threatening and they were at his house in Malibu, he'd plan a romantic picnic on the beach. Chilly wind hit his face, making him miss the warm, salty sea breeze. *Man, you've gone soft.*

He hadn't lived full time in Montana since leaving for basic training. Back then, he assumed going into the military was like winning the consolation trophy. He might have given up the dream of playing professional football but never lost the desire to be successful. In the end, he'd left the military with what he'd wanted from the endeavor, with the exception of a broken femur. The skills he'd learned from serving helped craft his business. Resilience and toughness had been ingrained into him by Pops at an early age, but the army refined them. He'd assumed wealthier clients, bigger clients, would provide fulfillment. Even the newest one, his company's highest-dollar-value contract yet, left him searching for more. Had he been racing toward the wrong goal his entire adult life?

When evaluating a protection assignment, Nicolas defined the client, any and all possible threats, and the intended locations. In his current situation, he used those same criteria. The people behind the threat were still hiding in the shadows. He'd remain flexible because, as the last several days proved, anything could happen. Hope for the best and expect the worst.

Arms sore, he swung the axe in a downward motion and stuck the blade in a log. While adding the newly chopped wood to a pile meant for drying, he considered the puzzle pieces Trevor had left behind. Manny, a guy who'd been a friend of Trevor's, was in business with the cartel. He also appeared to be offering the cartel's money for loans with the gains of interest adding to his profits. Had the cartel discovered Manny's side business? Had someone come up short on repayment to Manny and pressure had been applied? Enough pressure to commit a robbery and frame Trevor? If so, then how was Trevor involved? Nicolas struggled to accept that Trevor was involved in anything illegal. Why go through all the effort of contacting Nicolas, someone who'd been injured by events a decade and a half ago, if Trevor hadn't meant his apology?

The questions made his head hurt. If only they could decipher the ledger, then they'd understand the scope of Manny's operation. An idea struck. He trudged through the knee-high snow drift and onto the porch. A glance inside showed Hillary knitting while Olive snuggled with Sasha on the sofa, watching a movie. Farther in, Kayla sat at the kitchen table, back facing him. Likely still hunched over the ledger, studying it.

Before opening the door, he took a moment to soak in his surroundings. The snowfall had eased throughout the day while the wind remained strong and whipped top layers of snow off the ground and sent them into the air like white missiles. His gaze lifted toward the tree line to the north where the echoes of limbs cracked in the woods. Spruce trees dominated the area, and their branches covered in ever-present needles were no match for the weight of collecting snow.

Nicolas stomped on the porch to knock off most of the snow on his boots, then entered the warm embrace of the cabin. He dropped off the load of wood in his arms, then rid himself of his hat, scarf, jacket, gloves and boots. Beelining into the kitchen, he halted by Kayla. "What if Trevor had the key for the ledger too? He went through the trouble to copy the accounting ledger. Why wouldn't he have done the same with what was used to decipher the code?"

"I studied every page in here and didn't find a reference that linked the fake names with real ones." Kayla rubbed her eyes. "All I know for sure is huge amounts of money moved through these people's hands. Many times more than what the stolen necklace and diamonds are worth. What if the museum theft and this accounting record aren't related?"

"Perhaps." He considered the pieces again, convinced they all fit together to produce a cohesive picture. "All the threats you've received so far have been related to the stolen items. Nothing referencing this accounting ledger. But Trevor hid it for a reason."

"What infuriates me is that he hid it in Olive's bag." Both her hands formed into fists, resting on either side of the journal. "A good father would have kept evidence of criminal activity as far away from a preschooler as possible."

He agreed. If Nicolas were in a similar situation, he'd have ensured no link could be made between his family and items the criminals wanted back. Then again, he wouldn't have been involved with criminals in the first place. He shouldn't judge Trevor too harshly. The man was dead and couldn't defend himself or his actions. "He most likely placed the book in Olive's bag believing he'd hand it over to you along with Olive before going deeper into hiding."

"I want that to be true." Kayla pushed to stand with a *humph*. "I hate defending him. I've spent my life blaming him."

"No one deserves to be defended. That's the message of Easter, right?" He'd tread carefully in respect for her raw feelings about her father. "We don't deserve the grace we receive, but it's given anyway."

Her face lost most of its tension. "I don't like that you're right on a regular basis."

"Every so often, God smacks me on the head with a reminder of His goodness." Like the view of creation Nicolas had witnessed outside. The power of nature couldn't be ignored. And God had sent Kayla into his life again. Not the most ideal reunion. But he was grateful to be here in her time of need. "I'll search Olive's duffle bag again."

"I'll go through the rest of her belongings. Trevor could have hidden the other pages and index in something we didn't bring along."

"True. We'll at least try. Beats watching pony cartoons with Olive." He loved seeing Kayla smile.

"Great point." Kayla disappeared into the bedroom she shared with Olive.

He took the duffle bag and turned it inside out, unzipping the front pocket and swiping his hand into the opening. He came out with nothing other than a coating of glitter.

"Nicolas, I think I found something," Kayla called from the bedroom.

When he entered the room, the sight of her holding a sheet of lined paper sent his pulse racing. "What is it?"

"I found this tucked inside one of Olive's books. She had the book with her at the motel." Kayla flipped through the pages, staring at each with wide eyes. "It's an index for the ledger. And, I hope, the key to figuring out all the players in this twisted game."

FIFTEEN

Between the two of them, Kayla and Nicolas studied the paper, making short work of matching code names with the real ones. She knew several of the people listed. Inspector Cousteau turned out to be Sheriff Gomez.

"How can we trust the sheriff's department to do the right thing when the sheriff was taking loans from criminals?" Kayla pressed a hand to her stomach. The slice of cake she'd been looking forward to sat abandoned on the table. "Most of these names I don't recognize, but I know enough of them to make me uncomfortable. If this list gets out, a lot of people will be in serious trouble." Which begged the question—why hadn't Trevor turned it in? He'd had evidence in his possession that could have brought down the sheriff and other prominent residents of Snowberry and the greater area. Perhaps Kayla had answered her own question. "I wonder if anyone knows the ledger was copied."

Scratching his chin, Nicolas tossed his pen on the table. "At this point, we can trust few people. No wonder Trevor didn't go to the sheriff's department for help."

Her mind went to Christina—the only other person beside themselves who knew they were hiding here. "Did you find Detective Reimer's name?"

"No." He shook his head. "I want to believe she's one of the honest ones."

"So do I." But Kayla couldn't afford to blindly trust anyone. Not even an acquaintance from high school. "I'm reporting this to the FBI." She stood, then remembered they had no internet, and their cell phones and the satellite phone showed no service. She'd call on the landline but didn't know the nearest FBI station's number. If she dialed zero, would she reach an operator?

Kayla lifted up the receiver and held it to her ear. Silence. She tapped the lever on the body of the phone with no dial tone. "The phone lines must have been knocked out by the storm. We have no contact with the outside world."

Panic struck, and dizziness tipped the kitchen floor underneath her feet. They were stuck with no means of communication. The satellite phone had been ineffective so far. If the storm trapped them in the cabin, then it followed that the bad weather would keep others away. The pessimistic part of her still worried. "Let's make sure all the guns in the house are loaded, locked away for Olive's safety, but ready if needed."

Nightmares haunted Kayla's sleep. She gave up at 5:00 a.m. and slipped out of bed, careful not to wake Olive and Sasha. Walking with soft footsteps, she went to the bathroom, then headed into the living room, where she found Nicolas sitting in the recliner, staring outside into the darkness.

"Good morning," she spoke in a low voice. Exhaustion clogged her throat. "You couldn't sleep either?"

He turned his gaze from the window to Kayla. "Gave up around two o'clock. I stepped outside and checked the satellite phone. Still no signal."

"The snow has picked up again." Her observation made the warm comfort of the cabin seem more pleasurable. April snowstorms were rare, but history had recorded one of Montana's worst in 1969. Mountain weather could be wildly unpredictable. They had no choice but to ride out this storm.

"I'll make breakfast." Nicolas stood and stretched his arms overhead. "What's your fancy?"

Good-looking and talented in the kitchen. A nice combo to have around the house. "Fried eggs and toast. I'll start the coffee."

Nicolas worked the stove and toaster while she sat at the table sipping her coffee and observing as he went about his tasks. Soon, a plate was placed on the table, steaming with two eggs with bright yellow centers and two slices of jam-covered toast.

"Thank you." She pierced an egg with the tines of her fork. "My favorite meal is one I didn't make."

He chuckled and dug into his own full plate of food.

By the time they'd finished, the soft light of dawn had broken through the gloom. The sun stayed hidden behind storm clouds, but she knew it was there, just as she had faith God hadn't abandoned them.

Kayla's mom appeared, bleary-eyed but alert. "Who made breakfast already this morning?"

Nicolas raised a hand. "I cooked eggs and toast. Nothing fancy. Do you want me to put something together for you?"

"That would be lovely. Thank you."

"I'd bet a hundred dollars she wouldn't take me up on an offer to make breakfast," said Kayla. The teasing helped lift some of the heavy mood that had settled over them since discovering the accounting ledger and index. Knowing how deep the corruption went poisoned her faith in those entrusted with her family's safety.

Once Olive was up and fed and Sasha let outside then given food and water, Kayla took a shower and dressed. She'd been at the cabin for less than forty-eight hours and gained a visceral understanding of the term *cabin fever*. It was cold and snowy, and yesterday they'd seen a grizzly bear, but she had to breathe fresh air and walk in nature. A short break would clear her head and settle her soul.

Olive had settled on the sofa with Sasha to watch another pony cartoon. Given the circumstances, TV provided a diversion. Once their life returned to normal, or at least more normal than it currently was, Kayla promised to make up for all the TV time with trips to parks and other fun activities together.

"Can I join you?" Nicolas asked while sliding on a stocking hat.

"Of course." She tied her boot and checked in with her mom before heading out. "Bar the door behind us.

We won't be gone long, and we'll stay within view of the cabin."

Tucking his handgun in the holster underneath his coat, Nicolas observed their surroundings. "Rather be safe than sorry."

"I hate expecting danger to pop out from behind the trees at any second." She stepped down off the porch and her boots sank into more than a foot of snow. A break in the gray clouds allowed a ray of sun to cast a section of the lake in warmth. The cabin sat on ten acres with the shore of Talbot Lake a short distance from the cabin's front door. A dock extended from the land and over the water. The lake was a small, private body of water with only a couple other cottages on its shore. A layer of ice remained along the shoreline, emerging about twenty feet to meet open water. Soon, warmer weather would melt any remnants of winter.

"You've been incredibly brave through all this." Nicolas trudged along the footpath leading down to the lake. "Tell me about your life. We knew each other well in high school, and I'm angry at myself for letting that slip away."

"You can't take all the blame. I could have reached out to you before we graduated." She stopped on the rocky area where land met frozen water and glanced at Nicolas, who stood close. She'd been attracted to him, and truth be told, she still was. Shutting down those feelings proved to be difficult in their current situation.

He rubbed the back of his neck. "I thought we agreed to bury that part of our history."

"You're right. No more guilt and blame." She vowed

once and for all let go of the negative emotions tied to their past. If only she could stop herself from shutting down to protect herself. A defense mechanism learned from a traumatic childhood. Breaking down the walls around her heart would be difficult but not impossible. She'd stick with comfortable, easy subjects. "I went to Colorado State for college, fell in love with the area and decided to stay." An easy decision to make. She could live as Kayla Swartz without the stain of her association to Trevor. The Swartz name didn't mean anything different than the other thousands of last names. "I teach high school art, and Sasha and I visit the children's wards at several local hospitals. Sasha is a great therapy dog, and the kids love her."

"She's been the perfect companion for Olive."

"Dogs read human emotion better than people." She watched an eagle soar high over the surface of the water. "Other than teaching and working with Sasha, my life is fairly boring." She never thought her boring, predicable life would be swept away by theft and murder, yet it had been. Kayla looked forward to getting her boring existence back. Moving away from the lake, she hiked up to the driveway.

Nicolas kept at her side. "What you do is admirable. I wish I could say the same."

"You protect people. That's admirable too." She glanced over her shoulder at the cabin. They'd traveled up the driveway and over to a section of a wooded area that circled the building in a U shape. More sunbeams were cutting through the clouds, highlighting parts of the cabin's red metal roof.

"I protect rich people for money," Nicolas said. "I'm not winning any humanitarian awards for that."

"During our tutoring sessions, you promised you'd leave Snowberry and be successful. You should be proud that you accomplished your goal. I am." In high school, she'd dreamed of going with him and being a part of his success. She'd witnessed the fire that burned inside him, one that wanted to grow into something more than the small, rural town of Snowberry would allow.

"Success means different things to different people." He kicked up snow with the tip of his boot. "Making a name for myself meant I accomplished what I'd set out to do. If I'm honest, my business has made me a lot of money, but there's still a hole inside me. I've never admitted that to anyone before."

His confession felt familiar. During their tutoring sessions, they'd shared experiences and feelings spoken to no one else. "Money never can be a substitute for fulfilling your life's mission." She'd found her mission the first time she witnessed her golden retriever puppy be drawn to a child in a wheelchair at the park. Sasha instinctively had known how to provide comfort and joy. After a year of training for both of them, Kayla and Sasha graduated as a team.

"You're right, of course. I felt part of a mission while serving in the army. My military career ended sooner than I wanted." He tapped his left thigh.

"What happened?"

One corner of his mouth lifted. "Would you believe I stepped into the middle of something that didn't involve me? A buddy of mine and another soldier were throwing insults back and forth during a training exercise in Guatemala. We'd been tasked with improving the shooting skills of the local military force, but we were not doing well demonstrating teamwork. I tried to deescalate the argument, and before I knew it, the other soldier discharged his weapon into my leg."

She gazed up at him slack-jawed. "Another soldier shot you?"

"Not on purpose. It took a while, but I fully healed and rebuilt the strength in my leg." He shrugged. "The point is that breaking my arm during the bar fight wasn't the only instance of when I was injured for not minding my own business. It's in my blood, I guess."

And now he was here with her. Defending her family even though he had no reason to be involved. *Please don't let him be hurt again.* The next time, he might not survive. A freezing sensation traveled up her spine.

"I can read your mind." Nicolas wrapped his arms around her. The bulk of their jackets made connecting too close impossible. "Don't worry about me."

Being near him scrambled her senses. "Of course I'm worried. I feel responsible."

His smile widened. "I'll be fine. We'll all be fine. Once we turn over the evidence to federal law enforcement, they'll catch the bad guys, and we can all go back to our regular lives."

Instead of improving her mood, the reminder he'd return to California and the business he'd built deflated her. Reality waited for them both.

She gazed into the forest. Full-bodied evergreen trees stood like tall, broad soldiers. Her attention lowered to the ground. The impression of footsteps tracked from along the driveway, coming from the road, into the tree line and leading into the woods. Eventually, they disappeared out of sight. "Did you walk through here?"

Nicolas glanced to where she pointed. "No. Those look recent."

"Older ones would be covered in fresh snow." Heart racing, Kayla took careful steps to the trail, then walked alongside it for a few hundred feet. "I wonder where it ends?"

"This is the direction we drove from. We passed a neighboring cabin about two miles from ours." He bent down and examined a foot imprint. "They could be from someone staying at a nearby cabin. They could have taken a hike, seen our cabin, and headed home."

"A stretch of a theory. Why head back through the woods and not take the road?" Since finding Trevor's dead body, she'd experienced growing paranoia. The sharp-toothed monsters she'd feared growing up had turned out to be real.

Nicolas removed his gun from under his coat and held it at the ready. "Go back to the cabin. Make sure your mom and Olive are okay. I'll look around, then meet you inside."

Her instinct to stay with him clashed against her concern for her family. "Don't stay out long. Shout if you find something or need help."

He gave her a brisk nod.

She jogged in the direction of the cabin, huffing with the effort of moving fast through the snow. Catching sight of her mom standing by a side window of the cabin, she opened her mouth to yell out to her. Realization dawned that the figure was not her mom, and Kayla halted in a flash.

The person, alerted to Kayla's approach, took off in a dash.

She gave pursuit. "Stop," she cried, even though the odds of compliance were none.

Ducking behind the cover of a spruce, the person disappeared from view. They were dressed in baggy clothes and a hood from a sweatshirt provided both cover and shadow over their facial features.

The bang of a gunshot dropped her to her knees.

"Give me what's mine, or you'll never see the little girl again." Another gunshot followed the shouted instructions.

"Kayla," Nicolas yelled, still a distance away. "Stay down." He ran toward her, gun drawn and pointed into the trees.

She intended to follow his directions until she detected the shooter moving in the direction of the lake. The form wove through the trees with surprising speed. What was the plan to get away?

The hum of a motor provided the answer. A small aluminum boat came into view, then the driver cut the engine. It bobbed in the water feet from the edge of the ice. The recent warm weather had melted most of the ice, but fragments remained.

Kayla would not let this person get away. She couldn't. With adrenaline flowing through her veins, she battled through the snow with the hope of cutting off the shooter's access to the dock. Unfortunately, she wasn't quick enough.

As the shooter stepped onto the dock, the driver gingerly directed the boat so the bow touched it. Once the shooter reached the end, they lowered themselves off the end of the dock and into the boat.

Kayla maintained her chase. She had to get a look at their faces. The person in the hoodie faced away, as did the boat's driver. They drifted away from the dock and farther into the water. "Hey," she screamed. "I don't have *anything* of yours. Leave us alone." They could not get away. With Kayla's attention on the boat, she moved too quickly and without caution. Her foot hit a slick spot, and she tumbled off the dock and into the freezing water.

SIXTEEN

Kayla, no." Nicolas raced toward the lake. In a flash, the driver shifted the boat into reverse, traveled back far enough to make a turn, then took off as quickly as its small engine could manage.

"Kayla!" His voice carried away in the wind. One instant she was in view, and the next she'd vanished into the water.

He ran faster than he'd thought possible. His feet hit the dock, and he proceeded across the slippery planks. The sight of Kayla splashing in the water sent adrenaline pumping.

The boat and its occupants faded from view. They were no longer a priority. Getting Kayla out of the bitter cold lake was.

"Help!" She called out in a breathless voice.

"There's a sheet of ice a foot away. Can you get to the edge and hold on?" He lowered onto his stomach and extended his hand. She was just out of reach.

"I'm sinking." Her head dipped underwater before reemerging a moment later. Waves rippled from her splashing.

"Keep fighting. Don't give up." How thick was the ice at the edge of the dock? He could slide across in a prone position. Would the distribution of weight keep the ice from breaking further?

If he could get closer, he'd grab her hand and pull her to safety. Her wide-eyed expression conveyed sheer panic. Kayla's head dropped below the surface of the water again. There was no time for assessing and planning. He sprang into action. Kayla's look of fear would not be his final memory of her.

Kayla's lungs burned. She sank down in search of the lake's bottom, hoping it wasn't too far underneath her feet. When her boots finally found the mucky floor, she knew there was no way she could stand and reach the air. There were several feet between the surface of the water and her head.

Using reserves of strength, she pushed off the bottom. Her mouth broke through the water, and she gulped down as much air as possible before the weight of her soaked clothing dragged her back down. She strained to work her way toward the edge of ice. Her muscles had given everything and it wasn't enough. She couldn't reach the ice, couldn't reach Nicolas.

Images of Olive, her mom and Nicolas hovered into her mind, and her submerged body hovered between life and death. She reflected on Trevor and mourned that they'd never made amends. Her dreams of raising Olive would go unfilled. Who would care for her sister? Who would love her the way Kayla did?

Her eyes closed. *Fight!* Any energy she possessed

had drained from her body. *Fight!* The icy water numbed her skin and froze her arms and legs. *Fight!* Nicolas's voice boomed inside her head. *Don't give up, you have work left to do.*

The bottom of the lake settled once again under her feet. Her will to live surged. She bent her knees and pushed off with every ounce of strength she had left. Her upturned face broke through the surface. Kayla inhaled. Air filled her aching lungs. She attempted to obtain her bearings before sinking again.

Her vision found the ice at the edge of the dock. Where was Nicolas? Something gripped her wrist, solid and firm. A tug brought her upper body up and out of the water. The tension didn't sustain, and she dipped back in.

Nicolas held her arm, directly under her elbow. He lay on the dock. His arms stretched out long toward where she treaded water. "Kick."

Kayla's foggy brain fumbled with the word. *Kick.* What did he want her to do? Finally, the mind rebooted. Now alert, she shot into action. Legs kicking, she willed her body to where Nicolas waited. Everything about her felt heavy and weighted down. The snow boots on her feet drew her downward like supercharged gravity. She wouldn't give up. Not when she was so close to salvation.

"Give me your other hand." He extended his arm and struggled to make contact. With a grunt of effort, Nicolas slapped his hand over her wrist. He had a hold on both her arms.

Her shoulders and upper arms ached as he hauled

her toward him. She took a break to regain her breath. Getting out of the water wouldn't be easy. Her teeth chattered, and her muscles trembled. Hypothermia was setting in. The condition wouldn't take long to overcome her in the frigid water.

"On the count of three, I'll pull you up. Don't wiggle, and let me do the work." The grim look on his face didn't dull the determined glint in his eyes. "One, two, three." He growled while lifting her out of the water, inches at a time, until her entire body was sprawled on the dock.

A cry escaped her lips. Relief gave way to the fact she'd gone almost numb and stopped shivering. If she didn't get out of her wet clothes in the next few minutes, she wouldn't make it back to the cabin alive.

Nicolas helped her stand, then guided her along the dock. Once her feet touched the shore, she didn't hold back her tears. "Thank you." A hiccup punctuated her expression of gratitude. Dizziness overtook her, and she collapsed. The beams of sunlight she'd delighted in earlier dimmed. Her vision darkened around the edges. The cabin seemed to warp and dwindle.

"Don't leave me." Nicolas swept her up and held her in his arms. "I love you," he said in a harsh whisper.

Her body grew limp, and she rested her head on his chest. The warmth of his breath on her face provided comfort. His solid body grounded her back to the earth. She barely remained aware she was moving. The clouds in the sky above parted, offering a glimpse of blue sky.

The sound of her mom's cry jolted her awake.

Kayla glanced around at the interior of the cabin. Focusing remained a struggle.

Nicolas set her down gently on the floor by the fire. "Take off her clothes. I'll grab some more blankets. We need to get her body temperature up quickly."

"I can do it." She fumbled to find the zipper pull on her coat.

Sasha shoved her face at Kayla, sniffing and whining.

"I'm all right, girl." She kissed Sasha's muzzle.

"Kayla, let your mama take care of you," her mom said, admonishing her. "I thought I'd lost you."

So had she. Kayla's thoughts took her back to those seconds under the water, when her life seemed to draw to a close. She sucked in a breath of warm air. The fire radiated heat, and she soaked it up.

Her mom removed her coat and boots first, then her socks, pants and sweater. She wrapped a blanket around Kayla's shoulders and another enfolded her lap.

Nicolas called out to ensure Kayla was properly covered, then entered with a pile of blankets. He dropped them on the ground next to her. "I tried telling her it wasn't warm enough for a swim." Picking up her wet clothing, he appeared caught between tears and humor.

Kayla found the energy to smile. "But the water looked so inviting."

"What happened out there?" her mom asked. "One minute I was completing a row of knitting, and the next I heard yelling and gunfire."

Olive toddled over to where Kayla sat and kissed her big sister's forehead. "Love you. You be okay."

Kayla's heart melted. "I love you, too, sweet pea." Her rage over the shooter and their getaway was balanced by the comfort that Olive and her mom were unharmed. "They found us and demanded I hand over what's theirs." She left out the part about the threats to Olive as the child was within hearing distance. "The shooter's partner drove up with a boat, picked them up and took off."

"Did you get a look at either of their faces?" Nicolas returned from the kitchen, holding a steaming mug. He set it in Kayla's hands.

Hot chocolate. How did he know exactly the right medicine? "No. I ran after them but couldn't get close enough."

"I was too far away to get a good look as well." He lowered into the recliner and rubbed his forehead. "I think we should try and leave. The storm broke."

"The roads are likely still in bad condition," Kayla's mom said. "And there could be downed trees blocking sections. Plus, where would we go? Snowberry isn't safe. And after what you told me about the ledger and Sheriff Garcia listed as a loan recipient, I don't trust anyone."

"We can try to drive up to the ski lodge," Kayla suggested. "It's, what, about twenty miles away?"

"I think the condition of the roads will be just as bad or worse going in that direction." Her mom walked away, then returned holding a hairbrush. She sat behind Kayla and began combing through her tangled wet hair.

The bristles on her scalp felt almost as nice as the fire.

"I can take a drive and check on the roads. See if I

can get the satellite phone to work." Nicolas glanced down at where Kayla sat, an unreadable expression on his face. He appeared passionate, both with anger and concern. And maybe something else—an emotion that Kayla wondered if she was reflecting.

Back at the lake, when he'd swept her up in his arms, she didn't recall a lot of details but did remember his confession of love. Had he meant the sentiment, or was it spoken during an emotional moment?

"Only if you're extremely careful and turn back at the first sign of trouble." Kayla coughed, causing her esophagus to catch on fire. The sensation sent her back to when she was trapped underwater. Panic tightened her throat, increasing her discomfort.

Nicolas knelt beside her and placed a hand on her shoulder. "Take calm, easy breaths. No one is going to hurt you or anyone inside this cabin. I promise." He glanced at her mom. "Keep the rifle handy."

Kayla suppressed her immediate instinct to push back on anyone making promises. Nicolas wasn't Trevor. Since their recent reunion, Nicolas had been true to his word at every turn. "Hurry."

He squeezed her hand, then headed for the door. As he exited, a blast of cold wind moved in, shut off by the closing of the door.

"I checked the phone," Kayla's mom said. "The line is dead. My cell phone isn't getting service. Here." She passed Kayla her cell. "Maybe yours will work?"

Using her still numb fingers, she opened her phone and checked the bar status on the top. *No Service.* "I wonder if we'd have better luck outside with our phones."

"You stay right by the fire. I'll step out and check. I can keep watch for Nicolas while I'm out there." Hillary grabbed her coat off the hook.

Kayla stared into the flickering flames, becoming hypnotized. Did Nicolas really love her? Care for her, sure, as he cared for Olive. No man had ever loved her, not even her own father. The question was followed with another: Did she love him? A resounding yes echoed in her head. *Best keep that to yourself. He's leaving for home as soon as this is over.*

Her mind circled around the threat they faced and who was behind it. If only she'd seen their faces. The man's voice had sounded familiar. His warning had taken her already elevated panic and sent it sky high. If only she could match the voice with a name. Knowing the enemy would not only help guard against them but lead to a quicker arrest once she handed over the evidence Trevor had left behind.

Kayla's mom zipped up her coat at the same time Nicolas barged through the front door.

"My tires are slashed. So are yours." He glanced at Hillary. "There's no way we're driving out of here. We'll have to either hike to another cabin or wait until Christina arrives."

"We can't hike for a long distance with Olive, not knowing if the cabin we stop at is occupied or even safe." She spun around to face him, her back now absorbing the warmth of the fire. "The people who took off in the boat can't be staying far away. My guess is they broke into a cabin in the area, then snuck over to find out if we're here and slashed our car tires so we're stuck."

"Sitting ducks is what they call it," Kayla's mom said. "I'm going to warm up a cup of coffee. Does anyone need anything?"

"No, thanks mom."

"Nothing for me, thanks," Nicolas said. "Tucking away his gun within his holster high up on the top shelf of the cabinet, he glanced at Olive, who played quietly. "I don't want her getting my gun, but I need to have it at the ready."

"We'll all keep an eye on her and make sure she doesn't go near the shelf. I don't think I can reach up there either." Grasping the corners of the blanket tightly around her upper body, she felt the chill flow out. "I'm going to put on dry clothes." She stood with care, making sure the blankets stayed wrapped around her.

His eyes closed and he exhaled. "For a moment at the lake, I thought I lost you." Nicolas raised his lids and focused on Kayla.

"For a moment, I thought I was lost too." Seeing the way he watched her, with emotions dampening his eyes, clarity struck. A near-death experience had altered her priorities. When all hope had been lost, she'd craved nothing more than a chance to live a quiet life in Snowberry, caring for Olive. She'd wanted her mom to be a bigger part of her life once again. She'd yearned for a future with Nicolas. Their first youthful romance had been poisoned by anger and guilt. Was the possibility of a second chance for them a reality or a dream? This entire time, they'd been standing in their own way. She'd be a fool to let him leave for California without confessing her feelings. But she'd be naive not to accept that Nicolas was better off not staying a part of her life. The selfless thing for her to do would be to let him go. Could she trust her judgment or her instincts when they'd led her astray before?

SEVENTEEN

No phone service—cell or landline. No signal on the satellite phone either due to lingering heavy cloud cover. No vehicles—their means of escape. Nicolas paced on the front porch. The landscape appeared peaceful, as if they were the only people in the world. The incident earlier with the shooter and Kayla had served as a stark reminder. Their pursuer hadn't given up. A snowstorm hadn't been enough of a deterrent.

Kayla joined him, handing him a mug of coffee. "All quiet?"

"Not even a rabbit sighting." He wrapped his hands around the warm ceramic. "Do you think we should try to hike to a different location?"

Her gaze hovered over the lake, where she'd nearly drowned only hours before. Did she recall what he'd confessed while holding her limp body after pulling her out of the water? He kicked himself for letting his emotions overwhelm logic. Judging from her demeanor, she hadn't heard his words, or if she had, she hadn't comprehended them. Maybe it was for the best.

When she'd gone under and hadn't resurfaced, he

imagined never sharing a moment like the one right now ever again. Nicolas had been poised to jump into the water when she'd broken the surface. He wanted to cry in relief, but the gravity of the situation stifled his reaction. Kayla wouldn't last long in the freezing water, and he willingly would sacrifice his own life to ensure her survival. Thankfully, they both stood on the porch of the cabin drinking coffee. He easily could pretend they were here as a couple, spending a quiet weekend in the mountains. Someday, the scenario might be a reality. Though he concluded a life with her meant walking away from everything he'd built in California. Living in Snowberry, or even Colorado Springs, required he leave important parts of his life. Was he willing to put aside his achievements to be a regular guy, the type of man his pops had pushed him not to be—a nobody?

But if he shared love with Kayla, wouldn't that make him the luckiest man in the world? He'd loved her since the first time he walked into their study room and saw her at the table sketching in a notebook. His heart had been stolen, and she'd held it since. He shouldn't have let her go without a fight after his injury.

Kayla sat on the bench. "We have no guaranteed safe route? My gut tells me to shelter in place. If we didn't have Olive, I'd think differently, but I can't risk taking her for a long hike when we don't know where we'll end up."

"I understand your concern." He wondered if Kayla was up for traveling a long distance on foot. The events of the day had likely exhausted her. "We stay and fight, if it comes to that."

She gave a brisk nod. "We'll fight. No one is laying a finger on Olive."

His admiration of her grit magnified. Every conversation with her provided greater insight. When he'd known her in high school, his opinion had been one of a teenage boy—Kayla was pretty and full of spirit. She'd challenged him, the star quarterback, when he dug in his heels during their studying sessions. Her tutoring expanded his mind and gifted him with visions of a life far away from rural Montana. He expanded his goals to college and a football scholarship. He imagined being an NFL star and living up to Pops's expectations.

"Where will you live when this is all behind you?" he asked. What was the chance he could convince her to move with Olive to LA? Nicolas couldn't picture Kayla there, lost in the hustle and bustle, existing around people who valued fame above any other quality. Did that make him just as shallow for profiting off those same individuals? Kayla had spoken about a personal purpose or mission. Until now, his mission had been wealth and prominence. How much longer would he find fulfillment on that path? Had he ever?

She exhaled. "My house and job are in Colorado Springs. I don't know if I'm ready to parent Olive alone. I could ask my mom to move. She's lived in Snowberry her entire life, and I was born and raised there. If not for the taint of the Swartz name, I may not have moved away. At this moment, I'm leaning toward moving back home."

"Trevor's name will be cleared." For Trevor, redemption would come too late. Not for Kayla, though. Her reputation, and Olive's, for that matter, were tied to their father.

Finding forgiveness would help Kayla find peace no matter the truth of Trevor's actions. Nicolas's journey with forgiveness had been imperfect and long. Holding on to grudges caused harm to both parties. His pride and ambition had hurt others and himself.

She gave a shaky smile. "You shouldn't have been involved in any of this. Do you wish you'd ignored Trevor's text and stayed away?"

"Ignoring someone in need isn't my style. Would I rather have bumped into you at the coffee shop, then hung out to catch up? Sure. I hope there's still time to do that." He'd ask her to dinner. Not a date. Not yet. If he loved her, which he did, he wouldn't act until he was sure. He pictured a nice quiet table for two and time to get to know one another again, away from the craziness surrounding them. But to what end? Once home, he'd jump back into his fast-moving life. In doing so, he'd drown without her.

Kayla felt as if a grizzly bear sat on her chest. Her anxiety had compounded until she wondered if she'd have a mental breakdown. Having Nicolas helped. Still, Kayla was a realist. Years of dealing with Trevor had taught her self-reliance. She had to rely on Nicolas because she had no other choice. The accumulating obligation left her uneasy. Her desire to put her complete faith in him waged a war with her long-held reflex to protect herself from disappointment. "Once we get back to civilization and hand over what we have to the FBI, you can leave knowing that Olive and I will be protected."

"I'm not abandoning you the second you make contact with the feds." He kept his tone neutral, but she detected a hint of exasperation. "There have been assaults at Trevor's house, your mom's place and the cabin. I'll be right there with you until the ones responsible are caught."

His assertion reminded her of the risk he'd assumed due to his involvement. "You'll pack up and head home." Speaking the sentence ripped into her core. Keeping an emotional distance was for the best. Though right now, keeping him physically close offered security.

Cheeks flushed with the cold, he stared down. "If you don't want me around anymore, I can deal with the rejection, but I couldn't live with myself if something happened when I wasn't around."

"I'm not looking for a savior." She paused to collect her thoughts. Her jumbled emotions weren't his fault. "Look, I couldn't have made it through this horrible experience without you. We're still in danger, I get that. Please understand that you have no obligation to us. You offered forgiveness to Trevor and came when he asked for help. Your involvement doesn't need to extend forever."

"I wish you'd stop locking me out." He lifted his chin and switched his gaze from Kayla to the glistening lake. "But if you won't let me in, then we'll say farewell and, I hope, stay in touch, if that's what you want."

Nicolas appeared hurt, and she'd done it. In an effort to guard herself, she wounded him. She couldn't help but keep him at an emotional distance—a survival method for her sensitive and wounded soul. Kayla's life would be anything but normal for a long time. Olive was her top priority, along with Sasha and her mom. Her sister needed her. Kayla didn't want to be dependent on Nicolas. Their flirty friendship would fade with distance, and she'd be left carrying a broken heart.

"I'll hike around the cabin and check out the perimeter. You should go back inside before you catch another chill." He treaded down the porch steps and across the yard.

No longer able to hold back, she allowed hot tears to flow. Inside the cabin, her mom caught sight of her and began to speak. Kayla held up her hands in a gesture to hold in any comments or concern. Sasha walked over and pushed her head into Kayla's hand.

"Go back to Olive. She needs you more than I do. I'll be in the room for a bit." She shot out the sentence before disappearing into the bedroom.

Kayla cried with heartbreak. She grieved for Trevor and that Olive would grow up without her father. She sobbed for every time she'd reached for something, and failure slapped her back down to earth. How many days had she visited her father holding tightly to the belief that this time he'd be different? He'd be better. She'd wanted him to change, pushed him to treat her like a daughter he cherished. In the end, all trust in her father had faded away.

Kayla wanted to believe Trevor was different at the time of his death. He hadn't stolen and done business with criminals. Once again, she found herself reaching for men who were a product of her imagination—both in the form of Trevor and Nicolas. How could she tell what was real anymore?

Lying on her bed, she heard voices coming from the living room. What was she doing, crying like all the disaster surrounding them only affected her? She sat up and grabbed some tissues to dry her eyes. Kayla could throw a pity party later. Yes, she'd almost died today, but she wasn't dead. Fight now. More tears could come later.

The deep sound of Nicolas's voice wrapped around her like a fleece blanket. She recalled the feeling of his hands holding on to her when she'd lost all hope. His strength pulled her out of the water. He'd saved her life. He'd said he loved her. Nicolas was real. And she had repaid him by shutting the proverbial door in his face because of fear.

Hopping to her feet, she rolled back her shoulders. The people who'd shown up at the cabin a few hours ago could return, and if they did, she wouldn't be caught sobbing on the bed. Kayla left her sadness behind and went into the living room to find her mom alone. "Where is everyone?"

"Nicolas just left to walk around the area again, then he's going over to the road to see if he can get phone service." Kayla's mom gazed into her eyes, pricking her soul. "Don't push him away, dearest. He's a good man and cares about you."

Her defense rose, similar to every other time someone attempted to give advice on her love life, or lack thereof. "We're ships passing en route to different ports." Not a bad analogy. She gave herself a mental pat on the back. Too bad the analogy was true. "I'm not disagreeing that Nicolas will make someone a wonderful husband someday, but he won't be mine."

Her mom made a sound of annoyance. "He may if you'd finally admit you deserve a good man. Every boyfriend you've had since leaving home wasn't worthy of you, which is why things never worked out."

"They didn't work out because everyone grew bored with me and found someone else more exciting." Her gut churned, picturing that scenario occurring with Nicolas. "How am I, quiet Kayla who's raising her sister, going to keep a man like Nicolas interested? He has an exciting life in LA filled with beautiful celebrities and flashy events." She'd trusted him before, and he'd left her to chase his dreams. How could she be sure the past wouldn't repeat itself?

"At least give him a chance." Kayla's mom wrapped her arms around her. "I thought I'd lost you for a while. When I saw Nicolas carrying you up to the cabin, my heart stopped. We all believe that we have a bottomless well of second chances. God's plans aren't always our own."

Trevor's plan of redemption had been cut short. No one was guaranteed another day on earth. She waited for her mom to release her hold, then stepped back. "You're right, as usual."

Her mom smiled. "No matter what happens next, we stick together. All of us, including Nicolas. He's part of our family now."

"I'm going out to find Nicolas and apologize." Kayla regretted her short temper.

"He cares about you too much to hold your stubbornness against you. Puts another mark in the positive column."

"Is there any on the negative side?" She was curious if her mom found any fault with the seemingly perfect man. At least perfect in her mom's eyes. Having known Nicolas in high school and spending many hours together, Kayla knew his faults as well as her own. Those insights only endeared him to her.

Her mom tapped her fingertip on her chin. "I can't think of one thing I don't like about him. Even the scar slicing down his eyebrow is striking."

Kayla rolled her eyes, then gazed around the cabin's interior. "Where are Olive and Sasha?"

"Playing inside the closet. I think she feels secure inside a small space." Her mom indicated the hallway closet with its door cracked open. "She wanted to make a secret hiding space, kind of like when she hid at the motel room with Trevor. I thought that was a good idea—although I didn't tell her why."

"If they come back, she'll either need to stay tucked away in the closet, or you can take her and run."

"I'm not leaving." Crossing her arms over her body, her mom stood firm. "I know how to handle a gun. Don't forget I have boxes full of shooting medals and trophies."

"Which is why I trust you with Olive. If anyone gets near her." Kayla's throat tightened at the image.

Her mom nodded. "I'll protect her."

"Thanks." Staying to fight wasn't her first choice, but she'd do whatever necessary to provide her mom and Olive opportunity to flee. God willing, it wouldn't come to that.

Kayla padded over to the closet door to check on her sister before heading out to talk with Nicolas. Little girl whispers floated out to where Kayla stood. She stilled and listened in, enjoying a moment of innocence.

"I got a secret," Olive spoke quietly to presumably Sasha. "Promise not to tell."

She received no answer, not unexpected given Sasha's conversation skills hadn't progressed beyond panting and barking.

"Papa gave me Hoppy." Olive paused.

Kayla pictured Olive holding up Hoppy to Sasha—purple stuffed bunny to golden fluffy dog.

"He made me promise not to tell," Olive said. "Hoppy has something in her tummy. See."

Leaning closer to hear better, Kayla felt the floor tip. *Papa told Olive a secret. Hoppy had something hidden in its tummy.* Could it be? Had Trevor hid the stolen jewels inside his young daughter's stuffed toy?

She had to find a way to check Hoppy and see if the bunny was carrying contraband. Dread shot through her. What if she found the necklace and diamonds? Meaning Trevor had stolen them and used Olive for cover. All the positive feelings she'd collected for him crumbled into dust. Had her father been a changed man at the time of his death or up to his same tricks?

EIGHTEEN

Kayla tapped on the closet door. "Olive, can I come in?"

After the sound of movement from inside, the door squeaked open a few inches more, and Olive's face poked out. "What's the password?"

A password? What would a three-year-old choose? "Hoppy? Sasha? Bunny? Eggs?"

After each guess, Olive shook her head. "Jelly beans," she declared with a giggle. "Want one?" She held out her hand, stained a multitude of colors from the jelly beans she displayed on her open palm.

"No, thank you." Olive must have snuck a handful of candy when no one was looking. A reminder Kayla had better watch her sister and the sugary treats closer. "Jelly beans." With the password spoken, Kayla was given permission to enter.

She snuck in, avoiding the coats hanging above. Finding Sasha seated at the back, Kayla lowered by the door and sat cross-legged. "What are you playing in here?" Her heart raced while she approached the subject of the stuffed bunny with care.

"This is our secret club." Olive patted Sasha's side.

"Is Hoppy sick? She looks like she could use some of Ms. Hillary's special tea."

Olive held up the bunny and studied its face.

The stuffed animal didn't appear bloated with valuable jewels, but she wouldn't know for sure until she had it in her possession. "Can I take Hoppy into the kitchen and make her some tea? I'll bring her right back after she feels better."

Seeming to consider the proposition, Olive tipped her head. Her curly hair created a halo around her cherubic face. "Okay." She set Hoppy into Kayla's lap with a sniffle. "Papa said to take care of Hoppy. I miss Papa."

"I miss him too. I promise to take extra special care of Hoppy." She lifted the stuffed animal and noticed its unusual weight. Since Olive always had Hoppy, Kayla hadn't picked up the stuffed animal until now. The evidence directed her to believe Trevor had hidden the treasure in plain sight.

With a heavy heart, she stood and left the closet. Olive and Sasha stayed behind in their fort, which was for the best, as Kayla planned to cut open the back of Olive's cherished toy.

She waved her mom over to join her in the kitchen. Nicolas was still outside. Perhaps he had found phone service and called someone trusted for help. If law enforcement could make it up the mountain roads and to the cabin, she could turn everything over and wipe her hands clean of this entire mess.

"What are you doing with Hoppy?" her mom asked.

"I think Trevor hid the necklace and diamonds in the bunny."

Her mom's jaw dropped.

"I know." Kayla had likely displayed the same shocked expression. "Is there a pair of scissors in one of these drawers?"

After a brief search, her mom extracted a small pair.

Kayla took possession of the instrument and set Hoppy on the kitchen table, preparing to commence with surgery. She took a deep breath and set the pointed tip at the bottom of the bunny.

"Wait." Hillary took back the scissors. "Olive will want Hoppy back without being maimed. Let me cut the stitches at the seam. I can sew Hoppy as good as new once you're done."

She watched her mom slowly snip apart the seam stitch by stitch. Soon, the opening was large enough to examine the inside. Kayla slipped her fingers into the opening and pulled out a few balls of stuffing. Another peek inside showed a black pouch. Her stomach dropped. The truth could no longer be denied. Her father had stolen from the museum. He'd died trying to guard valuable property instead of protecting his daughters.

Eyes closed, she extracted the pouch and dropped it with a clunk on the table. She lifted her lids to view the bulging velvet pouch. Unable to wait any longer, she tugged open the cords on top and dumped out the contents. Twenty diamonds appeared before the necklace. The array of jewels glittered like fresh snow. More than a million dollars' worth, that's what she'd been told.

Kayla was no expert on gemstones, but anyone seeing the collection would be certain of its high value.

The diamonds were roughly cut and in various sizes and shapes. She lifted one and held it between her index finger and thumb. The gem was clear and colorless.

Hillary took the necklace and held it up to her face. "I can't tell you how many times I've seen this necklace at the museum and dreamed about wearing it with a fancy dress to a formal ball." The necklace had been crafted for a socialite in the 1800s. The family had built their fortune out east and then moved west for land and new opportunities. The gold filigree design was enhanced with diamonds over the length of the chain. A large blue sapphire dangled from the center. The fastening of the sapphire held more diamonds—smaller ones that highlighted the sapphire instead of competed with it.

She set the diamond back with the others and ran a finger down the smooth surface of the sapphire. "Trevor gave his life for some shiny baubles." In frustration, she turned away from the wealth on the table.

"We don't know for certain Trevor was the thief." Her mom set the necklace back inside the pouch.

"Of course he was. How could he not be guilty?" Not only possessing but hiding the stolen goods. Trevor broke into the museum. Everything that had happened since was a consequence of his criminal actions. "Trevor didn't change. His second-chance tour was just another scam."

"Don't jump to conclusions." Her mom took a sewing kit out of a drawer. "I'll stitch up Hoppy before Olive notices."

Jump to conclusions? What other conclusion could anyone possibly arrive at? Trevor was the only person who'd had the opportunity to place the pouch inside the stuffed animal. He'd given it to Olive. Kayla placed the necklace back inside the pouch, then gathered the loose diamonds. Her fingers itched to toss every one into the lake. Yes, they were valuable, but they were not worth the cost of a life or the damage done to her family.

"I was attacked for this, almost killed." Her blood flowed first hot, then cold in her veins. "Nicolas could have been killed in the explosion, and Olive..." Her voice hitched. "What if they'd gotten her out of the house before we'd noticed. We need to get the necklace and diamonds to the authorities. Someone with no connection to Sheriff Gomez or anyone with direct ties to Snowberry."

"Not even Detective Reimer?" Her mom glanced up as she pulled the needle and thread through the pinch-closed seam. "You know her from high school. She seemed honest and motivated to find the truth."

"I don't have confidence in anyone these days. Present company excluded." Kayla had struggled with trust since she'd become cognizant of Trevor's lies and manipulation when she was a child. A father should be faithful and true to his word. Her heavenly Father had provided Kayla with a mother's unwavering love. But she'd grown up expecting the worst of others and failing to believe people's words. Actions could be deciphered by her mind as sinister, even those done with pure intentions. Which brought her back to Nicolas and how she'd refused to accept his inherent goodness. How could she fully put her faith in him when her life had been filled with disappointment?

"There." Her mom snipped the end of the thread poking out at the top of a sealed seam. "As good as new." She handed Hoppy to Kayla. "It's lighter now. Will you tell Olive?"

"I'll be honest with her." A young child Olive's age was capable of understanding more than adults gave them credit for. "But I also want to protect her. She loved Trevor, and I don't want to say anything to tarnish his memory in her mind."

"He tried to be a good dad," Hillary said. "His guilt about how he treated you motivated him to get fatherhood right this time. I don't believe he was the one who robbed the museum. He told me once not long ago that he wanted to make Snowberry a good place to raise Olive."

"How did he end up with the jewels, then? Who knows he had them?" And who'd tried killing Kayla and Nicolas to get back the treasure. "I'll find a spot to hide the pouch until we can make contact and report the jewels and accounting ledger."

But first, she'd return Hoppy to Olive. She tucked the bunny under her arm and went to the closet.

Olive was singing a song—her sweet voice declaring that if you're happy and you know it to clap your hands.

Kayla peeked inside. She opened the closet door and reached in, presenting Hoppy. "Her tummy is feeling better now. Ms. Hillary took what Papa put in there since it was making Hoppy sick."

Snatching the stuffed bunny, Olive examined it from ear to toe. "She says thank you."

She waited for Olive to ask about what they'd removed from Hoppy, but the question never came. Her sister returned to singing. Sasha had curled up in a ball at the back corner, snoring away.

That was easy. She'd appreciate the wins when they came. After taking the pouch from the kitchen, Kayla eyed the interior of the cabin, searching for a good hiding spot. If they had to flee and leave behind the pouch and ledger, she didn't want them ending up in the wrong hands.

Her gaze moved around the fireplace. The face of the surround and chimney were covered in river rock. One underneath the mantel had come lose. Kayla chipped away at what was left of the mortar securing the rock to the surround. She pulled off the rock, revealing a shallow gap. The pouch fit perfectly tucked inside. When the rock was set back in place, the loose mortar was barely noticeable. Standing back, she didn't notice a difference compared to the other fifty or so rocks surrounding the fireplace.

Next, she took the copied pages of the ledger and small notebook with the index and placed them in the center of the woodpile by the hearth. The pieces of split firewood effectively covered the books. Her anxiety settled with the knowledge she'd gained some sense of control over the situation.

Kayla peered out the front window. Nicolas wasn't in view, but her mom had mentioned he'd gone the other direction toward the road in search of cell service. After how she'd spoken to him earlier, he'd be justified in staying outside all afternoon. Should she go out and try to make amends? Trusting him with her heart would expose every vulnerable part. He'd see her fractured spirit and the sharp pieces of her defenses. Would he turn away?

She stopped her thoughts. The obstacles to her future with Nicolas rested inside her. The only question that mattered was: How hard would she work to overcome them?

NINETEEN

Nicolas shoved his cell phone back into the pocket of his coat. Technology was great until it didn't work. He'd gone out onto the road and held up both his cell phone and the satellite phone as far as his arm stretched— no signal. Not wanting to trek far from the cabin, he didn't hike up the road where the elevation was slightly higher. The risk of leaving Kayla, Olive and Hillary unguarded weighed greater on him than the slim possibility of reaching a signal.

Christina had told Kayla she'd drive up to the cabin as soon as the roads were clear. The snow had ended and the temperatures had crept above freezing, so he expected Christina could arrive in a four-wheel drive either later today or tomorrow. That was if no trees or utility poles had fallen across the road. Those took longer to clear than a few feet of snow.

As he strolled down the driveway away from the road and headed back to the cabin, the sound of a vehicle engine caught his attention. He paused, then turned, waiting for the truck to either pass by or turn into the driveway. He'd flag down help. Maybe they wouldn't have to wait any longer to leave.

The rumble of the engine faded without a passing vehicle. Could be it turned onto another road prior to passing by. He searched his memory for any intersecting roads near the area. None that he remembered, but then again, it had been dark, and he'd been tired.

The air was quiet other than for birdsong. His gaze took in the surrounding landscape. Trees, rocks and snow. Still, the hairs on the back of his neck stood at attention. His skin tingled. Years spent in the military had taught him always to trust his instincts.

He unzipped his jacket and removed the gun from the holster. His ears strained for any unexpected noise. A hawk took off from its perch on a high branch and flew overhead with a shrill squawk. Nicolas jumped. *Calm down.* A jittery man holding a gun was dangerous.

Without warning, a gunshot echoed in the distance, then pain burst through Nicolas's right shoulder. He dropped to his knees on reflex. His shoulder pulsed in agony, a sensation he blocked out. He extended his left arm, gun at the ready—safety off and his index finger rested on the trigger. In the army, he'd learned to shoot with both hands, although the aim with his left was weaker. His vision fixated on the point where the shot had sounded. He searched for movement in the woods. A flash of olive green caught his attention. Part of the shooter's body was in his sights. "I'm armed. I don't want to kill you, but I will," Nicolas shouted.

"I have no qualms about killing," a male voice barked in reply. "At least not to keep myself alive."

Still crouched down on his knees, Nicolas scooted backward until he found a secure position behind a large rock. *Please don't let Kayla or Hillary rush out at the sound of gunfire.* Eliminating the threat of the shooter would be easier without having to worry about anyone's safety.

The crunch of boots walking on snow alerted him to the man's forward approach. He rose enough to take a quick glance at who awaited.

A man walked out from his hiding spot within a cluster of evergreen trees. His hands held up above his head. He pointed his gun to the sky. "All I want is the jewels. No one would have had to die if Trevor hadn't gotten involved. Instead, I've been forced to chase them down. I'm done. Either I get the jewels, or you all die."

Nicolas studied the man's face, still a sizable distance away. He wasn't Manny. Was he one of the other guys who'd been with Manny that afternoon at the bar? "I'll take you down before you hurt anyone I care about."

"Nicolas Galanis." The man chuckled. "The high school's star quarterback who lost his chance at the pros because of Trevor. Am I right? Don't tell me his daughters are worth your life."

"Don't come any closer," Nicolas commanded through clenched teeth.

The man stole one more step before halting. He stood about sixty feet away.

Nicolas had a clear shot at him. Firing his gun meant killing, and he didn't take that action lightly. He'd pull the trigger only as a last option. Aiming at the man's center mass, Nicolas waited for the next move.

After no movement for almost a minute, the man lifted his chin. "It didn't have to come to this. If the Swartz girl had handed over what was mine, no one would have gotten hurt."

"Trevor didn't give her anything before he was murdered." Nicolas attempted to reason with him despite the apparent futility. He opened his mouth to say more, finger tense on the trigger, when the cold feeling of metal pressed against the back of his neck—the muzzle of a gun.

"Drop the gun." The feminine voice was unyielding. "Do it."

He lowered his weapon onto the ground with care. How had he not heard someone else approach? Their distraction technique had worked well. The movement of his arm sent pain burning from the gunshot. He grimaced. Warm blood pooled out from the wound.

"Nicolas," Kayla shouted. From what he could tell, she was near the cabin. Away from danger for the moment but not far enough. "Nicolas, I heard a gun. Where are you? Are you okay?"

His heart thudded against his ribs. The sound of the cocking of a gun chilled his blood. This couldn't be the end. He wouldn't let it be. But if he died saving Kayla and her family, he'd have served his purpose on earth.

Kayla heard voices shouting in the distance. The blast of a gun had startled her. She'd directed her mom to join Olive and Sasha in the closet, grabbed the rifle and, with caution, stepped outside. At first, her mom had resisted hiding with a child and a dog. Her mom was Montana born and raised, and wasn't one to back down from a fight but neither was Kayla.

She scanned the terrain from her perch on the front porch. The sounds were coming from the back section of the property near where the driveway met the road. Rifle drawn, she descended the porch steps and crept to the corner of the cabin. Peering around the corner, she sucked in a breath. Nicolas's large form was lying facedown in the snow beside a cluster of trees. He was a distance away, so she couldn't tell if he was moving, but the bright red path leading to his body and the crimson patch at his side incited horror within her.

Kayla's body was prepared to spring forward and race to him when she caught sight of a man and a woman near Nicolas. She froze, then jumped back behind the cover of the cabin. Her choices narrowed to two—go to Nicolas with rifle blasting or retreat into the cabin. If Nicolas was shot, he'd need medical care. How could she leave him? Olive's sweet cherubic face came into mind. If Kayla hid along with her mom and sister, these people would search the cabin, find it empty and then leave. But what were the odds of that?

"He's dead," a deep voice boomed. "Come out without a fuss. Hand over the jewels, and you might make it home alive."

Dead. The word struck her like a blow to the chest. Nicolas couldn't be dead. He was too strong and full of life to have his snuffed out by these cowards. Inside her mind, she roared. Kayla had planned to collect the pouch with the necklace and diamonds, hand it over and let them go. Not anymore. She couldn't let them escape. They'd be punished for Trevor's murder and now Nicolas's. Kayla pointed her rifle in the direction of the man and fired, intentionally missing but sending a message. The kickback of the rifle jarred her shoulder. "You'll pay."

After a moment's hesitation, she snuck into the cabin and secured the door behind her. A quick glance at the fireplace reassured her the pouch hadn't been disturbed. She flipped off every light, closed the doors to the fireplace, and joined the gathering in the closet.

"What's happening?" her mom asked. "Where's Nicolas?"

Kayla choked back her tears. She'd grieve once she knew Nicolas's fate for certain. For now, she'd keep a candle of faith burning. "We're playing hide and seek." Kayla spoke to Olive but knew her mom would understand the subtext. "If you hear someone come in the cabin, you need to be extra quiet. They're not supposed to find us." She glanced at Sasha. "That goes for you too." Kayla hoped her dog would read their emotions and stay still.

Olive clutched Hoppy and nodded.

Kayla met her mom's gaze. "Keep them safe."

Her mom grabbed her hand and squeezed. "Keep yourself safe. Give them what they want. You know where it is now."

After a quick nod, Kayla closed the closet door. Her options were few. She could keep the front door secured and face a standoff or allow them in and hand over the jewels. With Nicolas lying out in the cold, shot, she didn't see much of a choice.

She waited in the dark kitchen as the minutes ticked by. Then the bang of the front door being kicked in made her jump.

She grabbed the rifle, leaning up against the wall at her side and prayed for courage. If the need arose, she'd be forced to shoot and possibly kill another human. It was a task she didn't take lightly. She fought the urge to throw up with the sounds of footsteps from inside the cabin.

Holding her breath, she pivoted the rifle so the barrel pointed at the kitchen entryway. Her heart pounded so hard she was sure the intruders could hear it. She steadied herself. A man appeared holding a handgun pointed at her. She lifted the barrel of her rifle to stare directly at the threatening face. For a second, the shock of recognition unsteadied her. The stuffy museum director was a killer. She could hardly believe her eyes. Had he used Trevor to steal the jewels?

"Hello, there." Calvin's gaze scanned Kayla's face. "The sooner we conduct our business, the sooner your lives can return to normal."

A woman's voice called out. She appeared next to Calvin—Michelle, of course, his assistant. "The game is over," she barked at Kayla. "We know the others are hiding. Your sister and your mom." Michelle's gaze narrowed. "Save the hero act and give us the necklace and diamonds. No one else needs to get hurt."

Kayla wouldn't risk her or her family's lives over gold, sapphires and diamonds. God's value for His people was priceless. She remembered Nicolas lying still in the snow. Fury clouded her vision. Revenge wasn't the answer. At least not right now. The sooner she could get Calvin and Michelle to leave, the sooner she could attend to Nicolas. *Please God don't let him be dead.*

Lowering her rifle, she stood. "I'll give you the items that Trevor stole from the museum, but first, let my sister and mom go." She'd used the only leverage she had to ensure their protection. What if they took possession of the goods, then decided to eliminate witnesses? And since Olive had been present when they'd killed Trevor, she was a double threat.

"You are not in a position to dictate terms." Calvin seized her rifle, then gestured for Kayla to move into the family room.

"I have something you want and won't hand it over until my sister and mom are safe. Kill us, and you'll never see those sparkling little rocks again."

Michelle hissed. "When I agreed to this plan, Calvin, I didn't sign up for all this. Do what she wants. If you don't liquidate the jewels soon, you won't be alive long enough to enjoy the extra money. All I want is to disappear and never see this cold, forsaken country ever again."

Another wave of grief hit at the idea they'd killed Nicolas, and she turned the emotion to a sharp rage. A storm brewed under the surface. She'd keep calm long enough to safeguard Olive, Sasha and her mom. Once she was sure of her loved ones' safety, her fight would resurface. One thing she knew for certain, Michelle and Calvin would not disappear into the sunset with loads of money in their pockets and blood on their hands.

TWENTY

Let them go, and I'll give you the jewels." Kayla held firm. Neither had asked about the ledger copies or the index, and she would not bring them up. The accounting information belonged to Manny and his group. Calvin had borrowed money from the operation and remained in deep debt but wasn't part of it. She wondered if Manny even knew Trevor had made copies of his financial information.

"Fine." Calvin lowered his gun. "We'd never hurt the little girl."

"You tried to kidnap her." Her voice rose. Kayla thought back to the Easter festival at the park. When Olive had gotten lost and Nicolas found her with Michelle, they'd assumed Michelle was acting as a Good Samaritan.

"We figured Trevor gave the jewels to his daughters," Michelle said. "At the motel, he refused to tell us where they were. We wouldn't have killed him if he hadn't threatened to turn us in."

Kayla went to the closet and opened the door. "Get on your outerwear and take Olive as far away from here as you can." She leaned in close and put her lips next to her mom's ear. "Nicolas is near the trees on the left side of the driveway. If he's alive, tell him we'll get help."

"You take Olive." Her mom kissed Kayla's cheek. "It's a mother's job to protect her child."

"Lady," Michelle said to her mom. "This is a one-time deal. Take the girl and go."

Sasha let out a low growl, a sound Kayla had never heard from her sweet dog.

"Please go." Kayla rushed to the front of the house. She took Olive's coat from the hook and slipped it on the girl. "Ms. Hillary will take you, Hoppy and Sasha for a walk. I need you to look out for real bunny rabbits. Count how many you see and tell me when you come back."

Olive nodded, expression serious. She understood something was wrong. She must have sensed the danger in the air. To her credit, she remained quiet and obedient.

"Be safe," Kayla said to her mom when they exited out the door. "Get away from here as fast as you can and hide." The two people holding guns at her back couldn't be trusted. They could get the loot and run or change their minds about leaving witnesses alive.

Her mom had Sasha's leash gripped in one hand, Olive's hand in the other. "God be with you, darling." She moved away quickly with her troop.

Not wanting Calvin and Michelle to pay attention to anyone else but her, Kayla slammed closed the door and faced her adversaries. "I suppose you want what you pretend belongs to you. I thought those items were property of the museum."

"What need does a dusty museum have for a thing so valuable?" Calvin questioned. "Instead of rotting away under glass for the next century, they can be worn and appreciated."

"Don't you mean sold to pad your bank account? Is that what Trevor planned? To sell the necklace and diamonds? A million dollars would have bought him a new life." But why then had he reached out to her for help? He'd known Kayla wouldn't help fence stolen jewelry. "My father was skilled at a lot of things, drinking and lying being at the top. I never figured he had the smarts to pull off such a complicated robbery." She waited for a reaction.

"He didn't have the ingenuity to get past the security system. Michelle, on the other hand, is a genius with computers and was able to shut it down long enough for us to get in and out. To anyone monitoring the system, it looked like a reboot." Calvin's lips curled in a self-satisfactory grin. "I will give your father credit for figuring out what we were planning. He didn't arrive in time that night to stop us but managed to swipe the necklace and diamonds out from under our noses early that next morning."

She stared at Calvin, trying to read his face. Was he telling the truth? Had Trevor tried to intervene and steal back the jewels? In his final voicemail to Kayla, he'd said he had some things for her to turn in to law enforcement. That if he did, they'd assume him guilty. He needed time to clear his name. He'd desired justice. Given his prior criminal history, he knew no one would believe his innocence. Not even his own daughter.

Trevor had tried to do the right thing, and in the end, he'd paid for it with his life. Kayla's heart ached. Her father had been deprived of trust, and in his hour of need, she'd turned away.

"Hand over the jewels and we'll be on our way." Michelle moved closer, holding the rifle Kayla had earlier. "Cal and I may be history nerds, but we both grew up learning how to hunt, live off the land and handle a firearm. I may not want to shoot you, but I will. Your friend found that out the hard way."

Her vision blurred with anger. These two had taken so much from her—for what? Money. Freedom. Or something closer to desperation. There'd been amounts listed under Calvin's name, but only a small percentage had been paid back. If she had to guess, Manny needed the loans paid back to keep himself out of trouble. In response, he put pressure on anyone who owed him.

"What you want is by the fireplace." She marched to stand before the firebox. The once blazing fire had faded to a warm glow. Best get this over with. Nicolas might be still alive and need of medical help. Her mom and Olive were headed away and, Kayla hoped, found someplace secure to hide. Christina could show up at any moment or not arrive until tomorrow or later. And since the sheriff she worked for was compromised, Kayla's faith in the detective wavered.

Kayla found the loose rock and pulled it out. After removing the pouch, she tossed it to Calvin, who'd positioned himself directly behind her. "Now leave."

"Hold on a second." Calvin knelt next to the side

table and poured out the contents. "Looks like everything is here."

"She probably swiped a few diamonds." Michelle stared down at the glistening stack over Calvin's shoulder. "We're going to need them all."

"Everything Trevor had is there." She watched Calvin count the diamonds, swiping over each of them one at a time. "How much of this is going toward paying off your debt to Manny?"

His hand froze, and his eyes peered up at Kayla. "How do you know?"

She shrugged. "Lucky guess. So, is the cartel after you too, or just Manny and his crew?"

Appearing to have lost interest in counting, Calvin scooped up the necklace, then the diamonds. Once everything was back in the pouch, he stood. "I'll pay back what I owe and have money left over."

"To start over." Michelle tightened her grip on the rifle stock. "No one is going to find us. It's why I came along for the ride. Well, and to keep Calvin from being killed over not paying off his gambling debts."

"Shhh," Calvin ordered Michelle. "Tie her up so we can leave."

"You said we weren't leaving anyone alive." Rifle raised, Michelle stared at Kayla. "What if she blows the whistle before we get to the plane?"

Kayla's muscles tensed. "You already have Trevor's murder on your hands. Do you want to add more?" She didn't mention Nicolas. Partially because she believed he was still alive and partially because she hoped the shine of the jewels had clouded their brains of anything and anyone else. "Just go. Get on your plane and fly away. Pay off your debts, then sip drinks on the beach. I can't call for help now anyway, and you'll be long gone before I reach someplace with a working phone."

Michelle bit her lower lip, seeming to consider. "Tie her up. She's Trevor's daughter, and the man made a whole lot of trouble for us." Using the barrel of the gun, she directed Kayla to a wood-frame chair.

With a prayer on her lips, she obeyed. How could she fight back without a weapon? She glanced around the room for something to use, but she was outgunned and outnumbered.

Switching out the rifle for a roll of duct tape, Michelle encircled Kayla's wrist with tape. A thud sounded, like a bat striking a baseball. Michelle spun around, screamed and reached for the rifle. Someone else grabbed it first.

Kayla bounded onto her feet and let out a cry at the wonderful sight of Nicolas holding a piece of firewood along with the rifle while standing over Calvin's unconscious body.

Once Nicolas used the duct tape to secure Calvin and Michelle, he sliced through the tape restraining Kayla's wrists. Ignoring the pain in his shoulder, he held tightly onto Kayla. When her arms had wrapped around him, every ounce of anxiety left his body. She was unharmed. *Thank you, God.*

"Your mom and Olive are waiting outside." He glanced out the front window. The woman and small girl stayed by the lakeshore, away from danger but close enough to hear the all clear once he'd secured the cabin.

"I thought you were dead." She sobbed, her head resting on his chest. "Wait." Pulling back, Kayla examined his chest. "I saw blood on the snow. Are you hurt?"

"A bullet to the top of my shoulder and a nasty bump on the back of my head." The first thanks to Calvin and the second a gift from Michelle. She'd snuck up behind him, threatened to shoot him, then beaned him on the skull with the handle of her gun. His strike at Calvin's head had been payback—hard enough to neutralize him but not enough to kill. "If they hadn't been in such a hurry to get the jewels, they would have noticed I was still breathing."

Kayla stepped away from Nicolas, tears brimming in her bright blue eyes. "You were shot, yet you're standing here like nothing happened. I'm so grateful you're alive but unbelievably angry you were hurt." Kayla's eyes pierced Michelle with a stare that would have frozen Nicolas's blood if it were directed at him.

Calvin groaned. He attempted to move his arm but couldn't due to Nicolas's effective taping of his hands behind his back.

Nicolas opened the front door and waved for Hillary to bring in Olive and Sasha. When they'd come upon him, Hillary had realized he was still breathing and shaken him awake. It had taken a few minutes for his brain to start functioning again. Once he remembered Calvin and Michelle, he hopped into action. And now, they were all safe and the threat wrapped up with a duct tape bow for law enforcement.

Olive ran inside, followed by Sasha, then Hillary. The girl flew into her sister's arms.

The scene touched a section of his heart he'd kept shut. Truth be told, he'd closed it after the fallout with Kayla senior year. She could be the only one to unlock it.

He knelt and took the black pouch that had fallen out of Calvin's hand and onto the floor. Setting it on the mantel, he tried to imagine desiring the contents deeply enough to harm and murder innocent people.

"I hear a truck approaching up the driveway," Hillary said while standing by the open door.

Nicolas raced out with his gun drawn. He'd found it half buried in the snow by the rock he'd used for cover. The sight of a black truck with the sheriff's department logo heightened his alarm, until he recognized Christina behind the wheel. He put away his gun and stepped into view.

She was alone and climbed out the truck. "I couldn't reach you all, so I risked the roads."

"I'm glad you did. We have a present inside for you." He held out his hands to halt her entrance into the cabin. "But first, I need to know if you have anything to do with Manny's money laundering and loan operation."

Christina tilted her head and gazed at him with a confused expression. "Why would you think I'm mixed up with them?" Then a light of understanding flashed in her eyes. "Sheriff Gomez. Is that why you asked?"

He gave a quick nod. "His name was listed in the accounting ledger. I don't want to see the investigation compromised."

"Neither do I." Christina placed her hands on her hips. She wore street clothes, usual for a detective. Her gun and badge were attached to her belt, advertising that she wasn't a civilian. "I had my suspicions about the sheriff. After I spoke with Kayla about finding the ledger, I called the FBI field office in Salt Lake City again and was put in touch with a special agent who'd been working with Trevor Swartz. She didn't share a lot in order to maintain the integrity of the investigation, but I gathered Trevor was working with the FBI. He told the agent his hometown was being corrupted, and he wanted to do his part to make it safe again. Trevor mentioned that with Olive living in Snowberry and his desire for you to move home, he was willing to take on the bad guys to clean up the town. He felt he was the only one with the opportunity to do it. No one would believe he'd gone straight and was working for the cops."

Nicolas's instincts had been correct. Trevor had been one of the good guys. Nicolas escorted Christina inside and presented her with Michelle and Calvin, who were still bound and sitting in kitchen chairs.

"Here are your museum thieves," Kayla said. "With Trevor as the fall guy, they assumed a quick and easy escape. Neither counted on Trevor stealing the jewels from them. I believe Trevor wanted to hand them over to me so I'd turn them in. If he'd done it himself, he would have been arrested and convicted in people's minds."

Christina strolled to the other side of the living room where Calvin and Michelle were seated. "The museum director and his assistant. Such fine upstanding citizens of Snowberry."

"There are several names listed in the index that I recognized." Kayla entwined her hand into Nicolas's.

"Which is why there's an FBI agent on her way to Snowberry." Christina cut off the tape holding Michelle to the chair, then heaved her onto her feet. "I'll radio for backup. From the looks of your tires, you'll need a ride."

"If you have our thieves under control, I'd like to take Nicolas into the bathroom and look at his wound. He was shot." Kayla leveled him with a look, like he'd done the deed himself. "Just because he acts like it's no big deal doesn't mean I'm not worried. He should be taken straight to the hospital."

"Just a little blood loss." He rubbed the back of his head, which had grown a lump the size of a baseball. "And maybe a concussion."

While Christina completed the task of arresting Calvin and Michelle and taking them into custody, Hillary took Olive into the kitchen to make hot chocolate. The girl had stopped crying at the distraction of a treat.

In the days ahead, Nicolas believed Kayla would introduce a new routine to Olive's life, helping the girl feel secure and loved. No more hiding from the bad guys. Only good people from now on.

Kayla guided Nicolas into the bathroom and pointed to the closed toilet seat. "Sit down and take off your jacket and shirt."

He wasn't about to argue and followed her instructions. His entire body ached, and a wave of tiredness washed over him.

Sasha barked and seated herself in the doorway. The dog appeared intent on keeping tabs on Kayla.

Other than Sasha, they were alone in the bathroom. All the things he'd wanted to say to Kayla since seeing her again rushed forward, but his lips refused to move. Committing to her meant walking away from the success he'd built in LA. He'd become an ordinary man, unimportant to the world. Could he wake up every morning and be satisfied with a simple life? He considered the happiness his parents displayed. Pops had wanted more for his son than a small-town life. He'd pushed Nicolas to make a mark on the world.

The truth struck hard and fast. Those three words he'd spoken to Kayla after pulling her out of the freezing lake returned to his mind. He no longer cared about wealth or importance. His world had condensed. His future revolved around one person. He understood his purpose. After a lifetime of striving for goals outside of Snowberry, he'd come home for good.

TWENTY-ONE

"They told me you were dead." Kayla sniffled. She couldn't stop repeating the phrase. Seeing him there, seated before her while she cleaned his wound, she was filled with joy. They'd experienced many close calls during the last several days, and she thanked God for His protection during the storm.

"They used emotional manipulation to get what they wanted. I don't think they wanted to kill Trevor or me. Fear likely caused an eager trigger finger in the motel room with Trevor. Greed and fear fueled their desire for the chase." He reached up and tucked a lock of hair behind her ear. "The bullet didn't hit anything vital." Nicolas grimaced as she wiped a gauze pad soaked in alcohol over the open wound.

He'd be taken directly to the hospital from the cabin. No arguments allowed. Once the FBI agent took possession of the copy of the ledger, index and stolen jewels, Kayla could breathe easily once again.

"I've decided to stay in Snowberry." How could she even think about living anywhere else? Olive deserved stability, and for her, Snowberry was home. Olive and Hillary had grown close, and Kayla wouldn't separate them. The decision wasn't difficult. "I'll have to find a job here. Sasha and I can continue therapy visits. The schools can always use a friendly furry face. We'll have to travel a little farther for hospital visits."

Nicolas remained quiet as she wiped away the dried blood that had trickled down his chest. *Wonder what he's thinking?* Hadn't she misjudged Trevor and failed to give him another chance? Was she willing to risk the same mistake with Nicolas if he wanted another chance?

"Sounds like we'll be seeing a lot of each other then." He grinned. "I'm moving home too."

Her jaw dropped. Nicolas was moving back to Snowberry? Why? She dampened her expectation. Perhaps he wanted some extended time with his family. "Everything you need is in LA. Your business is there."

"Not you. Or Olive." Taking both her hands, he sandwiched them between his own. "All my life, I've been chasing dreams. First it was football, then the military, and finally a protection business. I've walked beside wealthy celebrities, had influential people drop my name and received invitations to dine with important people. Nothing made me feel as complete as I have with you."

She watched for a sign he was teasing. Instead, she found a serious man who was offering his heart. "What are you saying?" Kayla had to be sure. She'd misread signs from men in the past. Actually, she'd shut them down before anything serious could develop. She expected disappointment and therefore rarely experienced it.

This was Nicolas though. The man she'd loved since high school and had never stopped loving. The man she'd compared every other one against. He'd changed his mind about her once before. Would he again? Did it matter when all she could think about was spending the rest of their lives together?

He rose and pressed their entwined hands over his heart. "I'm saying I love you, Kayla Swartz. I'm asking to be a part of your life. I want to stay a part of Olive's too. I'm chasing a new dream, and it's being a family with you."

Her mouth turned dry, and her pulse quickened. She stood at the edge of a canyon. Jumping meant trusting Nicolas to catch her. "Are you sure? My life is complicated and messy, and I hate the idea of you ending a promising career."

"You and Olive are my future. I love you and can't imagine spending my life without you."

"Then let's get you to the hospital." Kayla straightened, flushed with heat and filled with adoration for the wonderful man before her. "I love you, Nicolas. We can't let your latest injury get in the way of our happily ever after." With images of a life together playing in her head, she grinned.

"Nothing will ever get in the way of that." He bent down to kiss her with the sounds of Olive's laughter and Sasha's happy barks enfolding them in love.

* * * * *

HARLEQUIN
PLUS

Try the best multimedia subscription service for romance readers like you!

Read, Watch and Play.

Experience the easiest way to get the romance content you crave.

Start your **FREE TRIAL** at
<u>www.harlequinplus.com/freetrial</u>.